The Billionaire's Hidden Heart

A Contemporary Billionaire Romance

ALSO BY GEORGINA SAND

The Billionaire's New Assistant Erotic Romance Series

The Pleasure Diaries Erotic Romance Series

The Bootleg Billionaire Erotic Romance Series

The Hardcore Hotels Erotica Series

The Submissive Pleasures Series

Available at all major online retail book stores.

The Billionaire's Hidden Heart

A Contemporary Billionaire Romance

GEORGINA SAND

The Billionaire's
Hidden Heart
A Contemporary Billionaire Romance

ISBN-13: 978-0692448779
ISBN-10: 0692448772

www.georginasand.com

The Billionaire's Hidden Heart

A Contemporary Billionaire Romance

CHAPTER ONE

Modest and sensible. That's the Maine character. That's the character I was brought up with. And that character was never more necessary than in mid-March, when a zero-degree temperature was a warming trend and spring flowers were still two months away.

Swallowing hard, I brushed the snowflakes off my face and hugged my mom, who was also modest and sensible.

Sensible implied you wore bulky flannel-lined pants, turtlenecks, wool sweaters, and long johns. It required you to give up the cute leather high-heeled boots for those big, but warm Eskimo-style clunkers. In summer, it suggested that board shorts and a rash guard might work better than a bikini. I'd embraced sensibility as a survival mechanism, and while it had kept me hidden beneath layers of clothing, and had also led to a kind of modesty, too, one that I'd become accustomed to.

And yet, today I was heading off to a big city, where I doubted modesty and sensibility would cut it. I knew I'd stick out like a sore thumb among the stiletto-wearing citizens of Boston, and it wasn't just because of my countrified clothes. I'd been raised in the country and was a country girl, whether I liked it or not. And I didn't know how to be anything else.

My mom sniffled and wiped her tears and squeezed me with all the strength she could manage. Then she shoved me toward the Greyhound Bus that was going to take me to my job interview. I bolstered my courage one last time and stepped on. My gut wrenched as the door closed behind me--I was leaving behind everyone who'd ever meant anything to me.

Still, I needed this change. I did. I was twenty-four and the time had come for me to strike out on my own. For the last few years, I'd been driving everyone crazy with my complaints about being bored and feeling like the world was passing me by. And so, when I won B3 Corp.'s photography contest and received the offer to come down for an interview, my mom and everyone else had demanded I go.

Somehow, I managed to push my suitcase and camera case into the overhead bin. With a self-conscious look at the other passengers, many of whom were staring at me, I sat down in that faux-leather seat next to a snoring elderly man with little round glasses. He jumped and his eyes snapped open when he sensed me sitting next to him.

I looked out the window and waved to my mom as the bus pulled away. She waved back, her face lined with a few new wrinkles, a loose cap I'd knitted for her covering her salt-and-pepper hair, her down-filled coat keeping her warm from a brisk wind.

Goodbye, mom.

I saw that she was crying again, even as she waved furiously. My own tears flowed freely. I felt like I was abandoning her, just like my dad had. She kept waving even as the bus drove out of sight.

I missed her desperately, already.

I tried not to think about it, though. I tried not to notice the way my throat tightened as we passed the You are Leaving Owl's Head, Maine...Come Back Soon! sign. When the last buildings of my hometown rolled out of sight, I wiped my tears from my cheeks and let my hand drop into my lap.

"First time away from home?" the elderly man next to me asked, his worn face creased with sympathy.

"Yes."

"Where are you headed?"

"Boston."

He gave me a reassuring smile. "I'm Harry Mills."

"Demmie O'Reilly."

"Nice to meet you, Demmie." He patted my arm in a fatherly manner. "You'll like Boston. It's a grand old city. Lots of Irish pubs, museums, and then, of course, there's the Bruins!"

I nodded and managed a smile in reply, but didn't say anything else. I wasn't in the mood to talk. Rather, I pressed my head against the window and watched the snow-covered hills and valleys pass me by. Maine natives had another quality besides sensibility and modesty: an ability to endure. We all did our best to have stiff upper lips, and not only bear whatever harsh conditions came our way, but also to make the best of them. I hoped this last trait would come to my rescue while I tried to fit in with city life. If I screwed up during the interview and B3 sent me back home, I'd need it even more.

My elderly neighbor sensed my reserve and fell back against his seat, too. A few minutes later, he began to snore quietly.

I wished I could fall asleep, too. To just get past this moment, this pain of leaving home, without having to experience too much of it. The best I could do, though, was stare at the trees that whizzed by and try to nurture that little spark of excitement inside me that wanted to come alive. The sky shone with a dull gray light, but every once in a while, sunlight peeked out, and I took that as a good sign. I tugged my coat closer around me, huddled down into the seat, and waited for the bus to deliver me to the start of my new life.

CHAPTER TWO

Hands clenched together, I stood at the window looking out at buildings that stretched impossibly high—higher than anything I'd ever seen before. The clouds and snow that had dogged northern Maine had given way to blue skies here in Boston, and sunlight blazed off the many-mirrored surfaces outside, to reflect against my eyes. The B3 corporate offices had to be on the thirty-sixth floor at least, and it gave me a bird's eye view of the city, the harbor, and every reflective surface in between.

I shielded my eyes and backed up a little, pressing into the conference table behind me as I tried to imagine taking a photograph of the city without letting the glare destroy the shot. Some of the buildings were simply amazing—at certain angles, they looked almost two-dimensional. Silently wondering how the buildings' architects had accomplished such a trick, I assessed different angles, thought about different filters...polarized or half-polarized—

"Demmie, thank you for coming down to see us, and congratulations on winning B3 Corp.'s photography contest," a male voice said behind me.

I spun around and found myself looking at a distinguished-looking gray-haired man in a business suit. Another younger man stood behind him. The second man was dressed equally business-like. My gut tightened—their highly polished appearance intimidated me. We didn't often see men like that up in Owl's Head.

We traded introductions. I found out that both men—Walter and Sean—were executive directors who managed the division in which I'd be working...if I got the job. Then they told me to take a seat at the conference table, and sat opposite me. We faced each other across an expanse of wood. A big vase of orange blossoms stood on the table between us and perfumed the air with a delicate, yet potent fragrance.

"First of all, let me mention how impressed we were by the portfolio you submitted as part of the competition," the younger one, Sean, said. "You have a knack for a creative photo, for making something dramatic from the commonplace. I especially liked the shot you took of the elderly couple sitting on the sofa. They looked so dynamic, so alive...so young, even."

Inside I was quaking, but somehow I forced myself to smile. "Thank you, sir, I—"

"There will be no 'sirs' in here, Demmie," the older man cut in. "Please, call me Walter. And this is Sean."

"Of course." I swallowed hard. "I took the photo of the elderly couple during a photography retreat at Maine Media College. They live at a nearby assisted-living facility. Their families were very happy with the shot, too."

"Well, it's genius," Sean said. I thought I saw a little flash of warmth in his eyes. "Tell me: How would you photograph, say, the vase of orange blossoms between us?"

I studied the bouquet and its small waxy flowers that gleamed like freshly fallen snow. Thick green leaves surrounded them, making their white petals seem even more pure in comparison. "Preparation is key," I finally said. "Choosing the right lens, the perfect time in terms of light, the best backdrop, identifying the focal point...there are so many decisions that go into a good photo. They would all have to be considered, and then decided upon. Also, it's important to find the unusual thing, the interesting thing. Sometimes it's not the perfect flower, but the bent or dying flower next to it, that creates a more interesting shot."

Sean smiled. His eyes became warmer. "You attended Maine Media College?"

I nodded. "I graduated last May, with a Master of Fine Arts degree."

"That's almost a year ago. Have you held any positions since then?"

"I've done freelance work, mostly."

"What kind?"

"A lot of nature photography, inanimate objects, some fashion." I pulled the portfolio I'd prepared for the interview out of the briefcase I'd purchased only last night, after arriving in town. "Here's my portfolio."

Walter took it from me and put it on the table between himself and Sean. Together, the men began to look through the best of my photographs. They asked me questions about a few of them: what had inspired me to take it, how I'd set the shot up, and what processing I'd done to the photo afterward. As I talked, I felt perspiration gathering beneath my navy wool suit—again, purchased the previous evening—and silently reminded myself to keep my jacket on.

Once they'd finished looking at my portfolio, Walter closed it and handed it back to me. His gaze ever so briefly roved over my body, from my sensible one-inch heels to the top of my modestly styled head, and his smile widened. I felt myself blushing at the way he stared at me. Guys back home had never been so...frank in their appraisals.

"If I may ask, is Demmie a nickname?" he murmured.

"It's short for Demeter," I admitted, my cheeks growing warmer. I fussed with the barrette that was holding my hair back, made sure it was in place. "My mom is an English professor, with a specialty in Greek literature."

"Demeter, the Greek goddess of the harvest." He turned to his younger colleague. "She's a goddess."

Sean grinned. "We've gotten lucky."

I smiled hesitantly. "The luck is mine."

"How do you feel about relocation, Demmie?" Walter asked.

My heart gave a little thump. Somehow, I managed to shrug. "That's what I'd planned to do--relocate. This is my first trip to Boston, but I like it already."

"Have you done a lot of traveling?"

"I've never really been out of Maine."

Sean picked up my resume and glanced through it. "It says here you're fluent in Spanish."

"I had five years of Spanish in high school. I spoke it well enough after graduating to teach it to kids at a Spanish language camp during the summer." I played with the edge of my shirt, folding and refolding a little section of fabric. I was really nervous, and this interview wasn't getting any easier. "My accent isn't the best, but I can hold my own in a conversation."

He lifted an eyebrow. "All of your freelance work has been for businesses in your hometown?"

"I photographed a spread of Acadia National Park for the National Park Service," I offered, some of my nervousness becoming excitement. Something in their voices told me they liked me. "I also worked as the primary photographer for Maine Now's online fashion section."

"We've looked at both, and we're impressed," Walter assured me. "You're exactly what we need: someone young, fresh, and with a natural talent that, quite frankly, is the strongest we've seen in a long time. We have a lot of Spanish-speaking clients, so your fluency is definitely a plus. What do you know of B3 Corp.?"

Suddenly my heart was beating very fast. "B3 Corp. owns a variety of boutique hotels around the world," I replied breathlessly, repeating the information I'd found on the Internet. "Also several restaurants."

Walter nodded. "We have a growing portfolio of restaurants and boutique hotels, as well as a substantial pipeline of properties under development and in negotiation. Our executive director, Natalie Selby, maintains the image of B3 brands globally, and oversees the production of all photo shoots: talent coordination, fitting schedules, design involvement, and participation in the shoots themselves. You would be working for her, in the role of brand manager. What do you think, Demmie?"

"It sounds perfect," I stuttered. Further words failed me. I felt stunned that they seemed to want to give me the job.

"What would you say if we told you that if you take the position, you'd be expected to leave tomorrow morning for Miami?"

I gulped and shook my head, then smiled widely. "Wow."

Sean grinned at my reaction. "I take it you'd have no problem with this."

"No, not all. After the winter we've had, a little sunshine would be great."

"It would be a temporary assignment, a few months at most," Sean replied. "You'll be working with Natalie on a campaign for a new boutique hotel that's just beginning construction. And you'll be getting a lot of sunshine, not a little. There's no one you'll be leaving behind?"

I shook my head emphatically. "I take photographs. I do my best to create art. I haven't had time for anything else."

Walter stood and held out his hand. "The job is yours, if you want it."

I stood as well. Gratitude made my voice tremble. "Thank you, Walter." I turned to look at the younger executive. "And thank you, Sean. I don't even need time to think about it. I want nothing more in the world than to work for B3 Corp." I grasped Walter's outstretched hand in a firm grip, and wished my dad had been alive to see this success of mine. "Well, then, Demmie," Walter said, as we shook hands. "You'd better head back to your hotel and pack your bags. A limo will be by at eight am to pick you up."

CHAPTER THREE

Short-sleeved shirts, linen pants, sandals. Men with dark eyes who moved slowly, casually, in no rush, their gazes falling upon me with lingering curiosity. I traded glances with them, these men who studied my gray wool suit and the oversized plaid coat that hung over my arm. With the women, too. No doubt they wondered why I was walking through Miami International Airport dressed like the abominable snowman. They didn't know that I hadn't had any time to shop before leaving Boston. And I hadn't realized how hot and muggy it would be down here. Within five minutes of getting off the plane, I knew I was going to have to make shopping one of my top priorities.

After assessing, and then rejecting, several drivers holding up placards with names other than mine, I found the driver my new boss Natalie had sent to pick me up. Older, friendly, and about a foot shorter than I was, Carlos led me outside to a Town Car and introduced me to a whole new world, one called Miami: heat, confusion, rapid-fire Spanish, eager taxi drivers. And then, luscious creeping flowers, palm trees that stretched toward a blazing sun in a brilliant blue sky. Orange blossoms perfuming the air with an overwhelming sweet fragrance.

Once we reached the city itself, I had only a few minutes to gaze up at the high rise buildings and cruise ships docked in a harbor before we crossed a bridge and headed into South Beach. As Carlos maneuvered the car along Ocean Drive, I shamelessly gawked out the window at the art-deco hotels, the barely-dressed people crowding the sidewalks and the parade of high-end sports cars driving past. My photographer's eye found countless things to shoot, and I tried to memorize each, so I could return later and do them justice.

Finally, Carlos pulled up in front of an entrance to a five story, sand-colored hotel decorated with chevrons and fantails. An art-deco sign proclaimed the hotel's name: The Barcelona. Giant palm trees flanked the doors and a bellboy in a spotless uniform waited beneath the awning that shaded the entrance. I stepped out of the car and paused to breathe in the moist air, feel the sunshine heating the top of my head and listen to the ocean, which crashed against the sand just out of sight. Somewhere in the distance, Latin music throbbed.

Miami felt so different from Owl's Head, Maine, that I might as well have been transported to the moon. Not for the first time, I counted my lucky stars. Even though I'd won B3's photography contest, I still didn't feel like I deserved all of this...glamor. Not a Maine country bumpkin like me. I figured I must have done something really wonderful in a former life.

Carlos retrieved my suitcase from the trunk and handed it to a bellboy, and then the bellboy and I were walking inside. I caught my breath as we entered the lobby. Two-story windows, soaring ceilings, rich mahogany pillars, granite tabletops and clean, symmetrical lines greeted my eyes. The feeling was understated, luxurious, like a rich man's study. I'd never seen anything similar up north. I wondered what other extravagances awaited me.

The bellboy headed toward the registration desk with my battered old suitcase, while Carlos joined me near the entrance. Carlos immediately began scanning the lobby, looking for someone. After a moment, his gaze zeroed in on a woman in a white linen suit. She was seated in a lounge area and had a cell phone pressed against her ear.

"That's Natalie," he said.

We began to walk towards her.

She had curly brown hair drawn up in a bun at the nape of her neck, and even from a distance, I could see she had a great figure. Her eyes were an animated blue and she was gesturing at no one in particular with her free hand.

"Oh, Miguel, don't tell me you're not ready for the initial shoot," she was saying. She paused, listened, then frowned. "I know the hotel's under construction. Tomorrow, though, it's going to be partly cloudy. Do you know how rare that is down here? It's perfect lighting, so we need to take advantage of it." Another pause, then, "I don't care. We'll be there tomorrow morning. Early. Have your construction workers bulldoze something else until we're done. It won't take long." She looked up and saw me coming. "One second."

Carlos and I stopped in front of her.

"Natalie Selby," she said, and held out her hand.

I shook it, feeling her firm, warm palm against mine and seeing the friendliness in her eyes. I liked her instantly. "Demmie O'Reilly."

She assessed me, her gaze running up and down my figure before settling on my face. Her smile widened. "Demmie. That's short for Demeter."

"Yes, it is." I glanced at the glass of wine on the table next to her. She was drinking already? It was barely afternoon!

"Welcome, Demmie. It's good to have you on board. Did you have lunch?"

"Not yet," I admitted.

She crossed long, slender legs and turned to a waitress who had just finished taking drink orders from a businessman seated nearby. "Get her a Cuban sandwich." Her attention switched to me. "You're going to need it, you know. It'll be a while before dinner."

I nodded, wondering what a Cuban sandwich was.

She gestured to a chair next to her. "Have a seat."

I sat and rearranged my jacket over my arm. I felt like I'd been caught up in a whirlwind. Hurricane Natalie, I thought.

She gave me a distracted look, held up a finger to ask me to wait, and then went back to her call. "I know, darling. It's not easy for you either, with your subcontractors screwing up like that. We're expecting a lot. However...I'm not saying you need to stay away all day. Just an hour, right after dawn."

She continued wheedling the person on the other end of the line, even as her gaze returned to me and she winked in my direction. I watched her for a while, then deliberately looked away so I wouldn't appear to be eavesdropping on her conversation.

My gaze wandered across the hotel lobby and I noticed a man near the bar. Six foot four if an inch, he wore a gray suit and had dark blonde hair which he'd clipped short and brushed to the side. Lean and muscular with an erect stance, he exuded power and dominance. A shadow of a beard darkened his chiseled chin, and a small gold hoop earring hung from his left ear. Standing there, with his legs spread wide, one hand on his thigh and the other around a bottle of beer, he looked like a pirate, ready to pillage and plunder. I noticed he wore a silver ring on his right hand, but nothing on his left.

I blinked to make sure I was seeing him correctly, then stared a little more. I couldn't help myself.

His teeth looked very white in his tanned face, and his blue eyes had an intense quality which suggested very little, if anything, got past him. Overall, he seemed remote somehow, as if he'd distanced himself from the rest of us. And yet, I noticed his gaze slide over to Natalie and stay there, as he considered her in an absolutely blatant way.

I shook my head slightly, cynically. Men. I'd rarely seen one as arrogant as this one—

Suddenly, he turned to study me. I froze, feeling the weight of those glittering eyes, and his close, almost insulting regard, as if he could see right through my clothes. I lifted my chin slightly, pointedly returned his stare, and then looked away, determined to show him that I wasn't going to faint on the spot because he'd deigned to notice me.

Seconds later, I snuck a glance at him, and saw he was smiling.

My heart gave a thump and heat flooded my cheeks. I turned away again, annoyed that I'd only managed to amuse him.

Carlos tapped my shoulder. "I'll check in for you,

Miss, if you'd like."

I saw the kindness in his eyes and nodded. "Thank you, Carlos. I'd appreciate that."

As Carlos headed toward the front desk, Natalie hung up on her phone call and sighed. "Miguel, he's very set in his ways, but he's agreed to allow us to come out to the construction site tomorrow morning and do an initial shoot, before his workers arrive."

"The hotel is still under construction?" I asked, dragging my attention back to my boss.

"It's called Beau Paradis, and it's being rebuilt, actually." She accepted another glass of wine from a different waitress, took a big sip, and savored it before elaborating. "It was originally built in the early 1900's. A hurricane took it out a few decades ago, and it's been sitting on the beach decaying ever since. Jon Baxter bought it for a song, or so he says. You've met Jon?"

"Not yet."

"Jon is the oldest of the three Baxter brothers. Together, they own B3."

I nodded. "They're quite brilliant, from what I've heard."

"Brilliant and rich," she clarified. "Each brother is a billionaire in his own right."

"Wasn't there a sister too?" I asked, recalling the research I'd done on the company.

"Oh, yes," she said breezily. "She's the real brain behind the business."

I smiled. Suddenly I really liked her.

She gave me a friendly smile. "Well, we'd better get you up to your room. We'll leave for the site in about an hour, so we can get an idea of what we'll need for tomorrow's shoot. I'll have your sandwich sent up."

We stood. Carlos came over then and handed me a little folded card.

"Your room key," he informed me.

I thanked him.

Natalie thanked him too, and then gave my gray wool suit the once-over. "I hope you brought summer clothes. It's hot as hell in Miami."

"I didn't have time. Walter and Sean offered me the job yesterday afternoon, and this morning I was on a plane."

We began walking toward a bank of elevators.

"If I had been you," she told me matter-of-factly, "I would have been in Loro Piana before the sun went down yesterday. You're going to earn a lot of money, so you might as well start spending it."

I wanted to tell her that until this moment, my values had included sensible and modest. Sensible and modest girls didn't spend money like it grew on trees. I didn't think she'd understand that, though, and knew such an admission would make me look like someone's country cousin. I simply followed along behind her as we hurried through the lobby.

"No worries, though," she continued. "I'll have something sent up to tide you over until later on. What size are you?"

"About a ten," I said, aware that we were approaching the guy who looked like a pirate. He gave us another flagrant once-over as we drew closer. I swallowed and tried to ignore the butterflies in my stomach.

"Shoes?" she pressed.

I blinked and hesitated. "Also a ten."

She glanced at me, then swiveled to stare at the

pirate. "Do you like what you see?" she asked as we sailed past him.

He lifted one dark, winged eyebrow, but otherwise didn't answer. Then his gaze found mine, and suddenly I was drowning in deep blue eyes, eyes that seemed to hold all of the mystery of the darkest parts of the ocean.

I gulped. They didn't make 'em like this up in Maine.

"Here we are," Natalie said as she stopped in front of the elevator.

I nearly bumped into her as I stopped, too, and forced myself to look away from him.

"Go on up," she told me. "I'll see you in the lobby in an hour."

The elevator doors opened, and I stepped inside.

CHAPTER FOUR

A little while later, Natalie and I were sitting in the back seat of an old convertible T-bird, with Carlos at the wheel. We were driving south of Miami along Bayshore Drive, with the sun beating down on us and the wind whipping my hair into an even frizzier mess than it already was. Somehow, Natalie had dug up flip-flops and a white halter dress for me to wear—frivolous things that I never would have bought for myself.

I had to admit, I was completely scandalized by the amount of cleavage the dress revealed. I'd always been modest, had always hidden myself beneath high-neckline shirts and dresses. Now I felt practically naked. Still, on the positive side, for the first time I wasn't roasting alive. Given the heat and humidity down here, I figured I'd better get used to showing some skin.

Natalie opened her purse and pulled out a bottle of sunscreen. "Darling, you're getting pink. Put this on."

I took the bottle, squirted some of the sunscreen onto my palms and rubbed it in as we drove through Coconut Grove. Carlos slowed the car and merged into traffic that led down a quaint little main street crowded with boutique shops. I returned the sunscreen to Natalie, then relaxed back against the seat and took it all in. Brilliant blue skies, palm and coconut trees, bougainvillea tumbling over walls, fountains spurting water—it was paradise.

When we passed a sand volleyball court, I stared at the players: four men, two against two, all of them in speedos that left little to the imagination. They were young, tanned, buff, their bodies covered with sand and no doubt salty, too. I imagined how they smelled: hot, sweaty, masculine.

When a blonde guy jumped to spike the ball over the net, I stared at the way his body moved beneath his speedo and blushed, surprised to feel a little answering tingle. I had more than a passing acquaintance with my most secret parts—masturbation was the one thing I did that wasn't modest and sensible—but I hadn't expected to be so affected by the sight of a man's body. I guess I'd never paid much attention in the past. No wonder I was still a virgin.

I sighed. "This place is amazing."

"Is this your first ride in a convertible?" she asked.

"Maine's too cold for cars like these." I ran a palm over the warm leather seats. "It's wonderful."

She smiled. "You're not doing too badly, for a poor little girl from the backwoods. Wait until you see the hotel. You'll love it. Beau Paradis has its own island, twenty acres of it. Back in the day, it drew more of the rich and famous than the Biltmore Hotel." She paused and pointed at a metal and cement bridge that stretched across Biscayne Bay to an oasis of green. "Here's the turn now."

I picked up my camera and focused on the bridge.

"Carlos, slow down a little," Natalie said loudly.

Carlos complied, and then we were moving slowly enough for me to snap several photos: the bridge, which gleamed in the sunlight; Biscayne Bay from the middle of the bridge; and Beau Paradis's island of tangled palms and vegetation.

Once we reached land, we drove beneath a streamer of blue triangular flags and onto a gravel road that might have been paved once, but had long ago fallen victim to the hot Miami sun. A simple wire fence on either side of the road kept us from the construction zone.

To our left, backhoes were clearing a large swathe of muddy land, and dumping an assortment of broken palm trees, rocks and bushes into dump trucks. Closer to the road, construction workers appeared to be pouring foundations and setting footers in the ground. Natalie pointed in their direction. "Tennis courts," she informed me, speaking loudly so I could hear her over the roar of the machinery. "Pétanque courts, a pool complex, a spa, private bungalows."

I nodded and snapped a few photos, then turned to the other side to view the hotel--a combination of old, crumbling cement and new steel girders. The old part of it looked like a typical hotel from the 1920's: perfectly rectangular, about ten stories high with rooms hugging either side of a main corridor. The steel girders were framing out a new, modern section next to the old part. The new gave the hotel a more sprawling aspect and brought the design into the twenty-first century. Beyond, a white sand beach and the Atlantic Ocean beckoned, and groupings of palm trees rustled in an ocean breeze.

"I like what they're doing to the hotel," I said. "It's the perfect combination of old and new."

"Jon—Jon Baxter—personally supervised the architectural details. He's a genius where that's concerned. I'll show you the plans tomorrow, when we get down to work." She paused and spread her arms wide. "I want everything done within a month, so we can open around Cinco de Mayo."

I glanced doubtfully at the old part of the hotel. "You're sure we can get it all done in a month?"

"We can get that done, and more," she replied, a note of steel in her tone.

Carlos pulled up to an area with a wind-tattered tent and makeshift picnic tables. A few construction workers in jeans and t-shirts were sitting at the tables, eating. They looked up as we parked and got out of the car. A few of them studied my cleavage, then glanced lower, at my bare legs. I fought an urge to hide behind my hands.

Get used to it, I told myself. This was Miami, not Maine.

One of the men had on chinos and a button-down shirt. He was talking on his cell phone, but when he saw us pull up, he ended his call and walked over to the car. He spoke in rapid-fire Spanish. I silently translated. He was very upset, because one of his subcontractors had delivered windows with defects, a broken seal of some sort.

"Stop speaking Spanish, Miguel," Natalie demanded as she walked over to him. "You know I can't understand a word you're saying."

Miguel switched to English and spoke more slowly. I remained standing at the car, feeling awkward, wondering if I should go take photographs of the site. The construction workers continued to watch me with a good deal of interest, and I felt myself flushing. I fanned myself with my hand.

Natalie paused to take a call on her cell phone. Miguel, clearly irritated by the interruption, put his hands on his hips. Natalie gave him an annoyed look and moved away.

"What?" she said loudly into her phone, her eyebrows drawing together. "You can't be serious." A pause. She pulled the phone away from her ear, stared at it with a deep frown, and then listened once more. "Son of a bitch. I can't do that, Nick. I'm down here in Miami." A pause. "I know, but—" Another pause, longer this time, and then her shoulders slumped. "Okay, I'll do it, but I have Demmie O'Reilly down here, she's our new brand manager for the hotel division—" She glanced up at me, and I could see by the set of her mouth that she was very unhappy. "No, she's not an idiot, she can manage by herself, but she just started—" Natalie sighed heavily. "Fine. I'll be on the first flight out."

I stiffened, my camera heavy in my hands.

She ended the call and hurried to my side. "That was Nick Baxter. He wants me to supervise a photo shoot for a new hotel they've opened on the French Riviera. I have to fly out there right away."

I stared at her with wide eyes. A tendril of anxiety wound through me. Natalie was leaving?

She grasped my hands in her own, gave them a squeeze. "I'm sorry, Demmie, but it can't be helped. When Nick Baxter tells you to jump, you ask how high. I've got to go."

"But...but what about this hotel--Beau Paradis? You wanted to open by Cinco de Mayo--"

"You're going to have to do it yourself, darling, at least until I get back." She started walking back to the car. I followed helplessly behind her. "Decide upon a brand identity and start working on it," she urged. "Take some photographs, put some ideas together, and email them to me. As soon as I finish with this other hotel, I'll fly back down here."

"But..."

She lifted an eyebrow. "Sometimes, we just have to jump in. This is one of those times."

I nodded unhappily and grasped the car door's handle.

She put her hand on mine and stopped me. "You stay here, and take some photos. Get a feel for the place. After Carlos has dropped me off, I'll send him back to pick you up."

Without waiting for my response, she jumped into the car. "Let's go, Carlos."

The car started rolling. Natalie suddenly looked back at me and waved. "Oh, you're going to have to take my date tonight. I'll call him and tell him you'll meet him in the lobby at eight PM."

I stared at her, my anxiety blossoming into outright panic. Did she just tell me I had to go out on a date?

I ran after the car, gravel biting through the thin soles of my flip-flops. "What?"

The car continued to accelerate away from me.

Natalie tapped Carlos on the shoulder. Carlos hit the brakes.

I caught up with them. Natalie leaned over the car door toward me. "I need you to stand in for me tonight."

"Doing what?"

She hesitated a second. "I've a date set up with an investor. We were supposed to talk about his initial impressions of Beau Paradis. I'll need you to represent me. That means you need to look and act your best. I'll have something sent up for you to wear. Fix your hair, wear some perfume, and put on lipstick, for God's sake. Be charming, answer his questions, and keep your ears open. The guy's worth a lot of money. But he's smart, and he's used to getting what he wants. So be careful. Got it?"

My heart pounding, I nodded.

"Good." She smiled. "Thank you." She tapped Carlos on the shoulder once more, and then they were driving down the gravel road, away from me. She turned to wave.

I waved back, and clutched my camera in my hands as they disappeared behind a cloud of dust.

What the hell, I wondered.

When I'd agreed to become B3's brand manager, I thought I'd be working closely with their superstar, Natalie. I didn't realize I'd be totally on my own. The truth was, I didn't know if I could come up with a brand identity on my own. At least not one anyone would care about. I was a photographer, not an advertising executive.

I would be fired before the week was out.

I sighed, squared my shoulders, and took a few seconds to give myself a pep talk: Find your stiff upper lip, endure, and make the best of it.

Then I turned back around, toward the hotel. I figured I had at least two hours before Carlos returned for me. I looked for the sun and saw that it had dipped closer to the horizon—which meant that any photographs I took would have a beautiful golden haze to them. I quickly decided to spend those two hours doing exactly what Natalie had said—familiarizing myself with Beau Paradis.

I trudged toward the tent. Miguel was nowhere to be seen, but several of the construction workers still sat at the table. They were bronzed and muscular from spending so many hours outside in the Florida sun. I wanted to ask them if it was safe to wander around inside of the hotel, but when one of them winked at me, I spun on my heel and started walking toward the hotel. I had no intention of flirting with the construction staff.

"Hey, be careful if you go inside," the man who'd winked called out after me. "It's a little dangerous in there. You never know what you might find."

I glanced back, nodded, then continued on. I heard him laughing as I stopped to take a few photos. I didn't care. I already felt down in the dumps over the thought of losing this job before it had even started.

A trademark. An identity, I thought. Something that would interest people. Excite them.

That's what I needed to find.

I walked slowly through the grass surrounding the hotel, past some drab, female peahens that clucked contentedly as they searched the grass for insects. I'd learned on the drive over that Miami considered itself a bird sanctuary, and that peacocks roamed free in small groups. Idly I wondered where the male peacocks were.

A warm breeze blew my skirt against my legs as I made my way around to the oceanfront portion of the hotel and gazed out at the ocean. I noticed a boat rocked in the waves by a decrepit dock. The boat appeared to be tied to the deck and, unlike the dock itself, it looked new, with a gleaming white hull and doors that led to a compartment below the helm. I didn't know much about boats, but the engine looked big to me. I doubted it was one of the construction worker's rides. It appeared too expensive for an average guy to own.

Mystified, I glanced up and down the beach. Saw no one. Continued toward the hotel. A large patio gone to weed encircled the oceanfront entrance. I crossed the patio and walked through an opening that had clearly once been a set of large double doors. All around the opening, square panels of green and blue glass formed an art-deco style wall of windows.

I paused, then stepped further inside. Took a breath at the mystery, the dilapidated majesty that greeted my eyes. The main lobby looked like a church that had long since been abandoned. I saw rotting beauty shrouded in shadows.

Beams crisscrossed overhead, with a ceiling at least three floors up. Steel pipes hung from cement posts, and girders reached skyward into the fourth and fifth floors. Some of the walls looked wet with moisture, and puddles of water gathered on the floor. I heard the faint sound of trickling water. Broken pipes somewhere? I scuffed my foot against dirty tiles and revealed a small section of marble.

I looked more closely and noticed other remnants of the past: art-deco mosaics hidden by years of grime, arched walls, a gleaming border of thin marble along the top of the wall, lit by sunlight. I picked my way carefully across the floor, through dried leaves and branches and construction garbage, my feet echoing against the marble. I walked toward a pool of light, and found myself standing in the middle of the lobby, beneath a skylight that had long ago caved in. I stopped and gazed upward. Dust motes danced in the sunlight streaming through the ceiling, creating rays that seemed brighter because of the shadows.

I felt like I'd stepped into another world. A long-forgotten time and place. I snapped a few photos. A mourning dove, disturbed by my presence, cooed. It flew out of the rafters and up through the skylight. For a brief instant, it was lit from behind with sunlight, and then it was flying free through a blue sky.

I took a photo of the palm trees that swayed just beyond the skylight, then refocused on the interior. To my left, I saw a wide cement staircase. I imagined women in sequined gowns and men in tuxedos climbing them to attend a soirée on the second floor. I closed my eyes, caught up in the moment, and when I opened them again, the hotel seemed even more mysterious, more beautiful, like an aging movie star who refused to give up the secrets of her past.

A tiny little thought about a possible branding identity came to me. I silently filed it away and glanced up to the second floor.

The staircase beckoned. It looked solid enough. I wanted to see the upstairs. I moved toward it.

A soft, distant moaning noise stopped me in my tracks.

I remained perfectly still and listened.

Heard another moan, and a deep sigh. It was coming from upstairs somewhere. I looked toward the stained glass wall, and the opening. Outside, waves lapped up against the sandy beach.

My heart beat faster.

The boat, I thought. Its driver was in the hotel now, with a companion.

I should go.

But I couldn't. I wouldn't. I wasn't ready to go. I needed more photos. And suddenly I was burning with curiosity. Who'd come here? What were they doing? And why to this run-down, abandoned hotel, of all places?

I checked to make sure my camera was on quiet mode. Then I crept up the stairs, one by one, carefully placing my feet so that I wouldn't make any noise. When I reached the landing, I stood still and listened. Heard trickling water, and soft, yet urgent whispers. The sunlight shifted, and then I saw a woman's shadow moving on the wall. I changed positions, and saw her.

I sucked in a breath and put my hand up to my chin. She did too, and I realized I was looking in a grime-covered mirror.

I'd spooked myself.

I waited for my heart beat to slow down and silently prayed the couple who had made the moaning noises hadn't heard me. A few seconds later, another little groan of pleasure floated through the air. I nearly sighed aloud with relief and moved in the direction of the sound, also toward a large hallway. Light didn't reach the second floor as easily as it had reached the lobby, and the hallway was filled with purple shadows. Keeping an eye on my footing, I snuck forward.

Suddenly, I caught a flash of yellow. I heard a soft gasp. I looked in the direction of the yellow and realized I was peering through a crumbling opening in the wall, one that permitted a view of the room beyond. There was a woman in there, a deeply tanned woman in a yellow sarong, with jet-black silky hair and a white lily tucked behind her ear. She was looking at someone as she sauntered slowly away, her hips swaying suggestively.

A man moved into view. He pushed her roughly up against the wall. She gasped again and crouched against the wall, her hands up and on either side of her head, in a gesture of submission. She was breathing heavily, her breasts trembling as they rose and fell.

I knew I shouldn't be spying on them like this. I ought to leave at once. But I didn't. Ignoring the flurries in my stomach, I shifted just enough to have a better view without revealing myself. I was shocked and fascinated at the same time. I couldn't turn away.

She continued to gaze at the man who'd pushed her. Her eyelids were heavy, her lips pouting. She wanted his violence, wanted to be taken. It excited her. Even I could see that. Though she remained pressed against the wall, somehow she still managed to strain toward him.

Suddenly, he moved into view. I nearly gasped aloud.

The pirate from my hotel!

I ducked a little lower behind the wall. I realized I was trembling, hard, and gripped my camera.

He was naked, completely naked, except for the gold hoop in his ear, and a silver band that he wore on his right index finger. His nude body looked every bit as athletic as I had imagined it to be when I'd seen him in the hotel lobby. Long, muscular legs, a firm round butt, a powerful chest, broad shoulders—he was a sculptor's dream. And his attention was completely fixed on the woman in front of him. He stalked toward her with the grace of a jungle cat, gripped the neckline of her dress, and ripped it downward in one savage motion.

Her breasts bounced and quivered. She moaned softly, her lips parted, her eyes very dark. I swallowed as I looked at her—she was perfect, with round, full breasts and a neatly trimmed thatch of hair covering her pussy. She writhed against the wall, then held out one hand toward him, clearly wanting him closer, but also playing by his rules, and remaining where he'd put her.

He stood there looking at her, his gaze raking over her as if he owned her. Moments passed, seconds that seemed to stretch out into minutes of tense anticipation. Entranced, I stared at the way the light was playing across their naked bodies. They were beautiful. Decadent. I felt a tingling achiness between my thighs as I watched them, but I paid it little attention. I was caught up in the spell that they'd created with their passion. I lifted my camera to my eye, focused, and took a photograph.

The camera silently recorded the image.

Without warning, he strode toward her and clasped her in a rough embrace. She threw her head back, her lips parted, and they writhed against each other, skin against skin. Their mouths locked together, and then they were kissing. He effortlessly picked her up and spun her around as he ran his hands down her back to her firm bottom, and then up again.

When their mouths parted, she gasped and entwined her arms around his neck. He pushed her against the wall. For a second, I saw his cock: big, hard, jutting. Then he gripped her waist in his hands and lowered her, inch by inch, onto his erection. She sighed with deep pleasure.

I could hardly breathe. I felt light-headed with excitement. Dizzy. I couldn't believe what I was seeing, and I couldn't turn away, either. Although I was still a virgin, embarrassingly so, that didn't mean I was ignorant. I knew what sex was, and what naked men and women looked like. I'd even watched a porn movie or two and had seen some pretty grungy stuff. But I had never seen anything like this...this passion, this heat, the kind that looked like it would tear them apart.

He gripped her buttocks and they surged away from the wall, and out of my view. Holding tight to my camera, I crept to the side so that I could continue watching them. He spun her around, and then around again as his mouth devoured hers; and then he had her against the wall once more, near a spray of water that was coming out of a broken pipe. He began to thrust into her, his hips moving back and forth, and she gasped, cried out. Writhed against him.

He said something quietly, words I couldn't hear, and they rolled around again, until they were under the water and it was spraying all over their thrusting bodies. The water formed silvery droplets that sparkled against their skin, and although shadows played across them, I could see the bliss on their faces, the passionate tightness, the yearning. They were so...wanton. So primal.

My pulse hammered through my veins as I watched them, a willing voyeur. All at once, I was desperately wishing I could be in her position. I wanted to be in his arms, to have him plunge deep into my quivering pussy. I wanted to surrender to him, I wanted to conquer him with pleasure.

I pressed my fingers against my lips, holding in a gasp as he held her up higher. She threw her head back and let the water splash into her face and rush down her body. He had his back to me, but she was facing in my direction, and I took another photograph, my hands shaking hard. The expression on her face was one I'd never seen before.

I swallowed, put the camera down. Ran my hands over my hips, feeling the curves; then up to my breasts. I cupped them, curved my hands over them. They were big and full. Sexy.

Their passion had infected me. It floated in the air, like some exotic perfume. Now I needed release, too.

I peeked out at them. His back against the wall, he was lifting her up and down, making her ride his cock. She clutched his shoulders with one hand and rubbed her pussy with the other, wiggling around all the time.

I kept my gaze on them as I moved my fingers to my nipples. I rubbed that sensitive, aching flesh; I teased them through the fabric of my white gauze dress. Then I pinched them, gently, lightly, sending a tingling sensation straight down to my pussy.

Holding in a moan, I leaned against the wall, positioned myself so I could continue to watch them as I eased the ache inside me that grew hotter and more demanding with each second. I pulled up my dress, pushed my panties down around a few inches. I closed my eyes and imagined I was the one riding him, not the dark-haired woman. At the same time I began caressing my bud, sliding my finger down between my pussy lips to tease some moisture out before gently dragging it upwards, over my bud again.

I remembered how he'd looked at me in the hotel, with those gleaming dark blue eyes, and I quivered with hot, desperate need. Breathing more quickly, but also trying to stay quiet so they wouldn't notice me watching, I stroked my bud with one hand, slowly at first but then faster as my aching pussy demanded more. My panties held my thighs together, and somehow, it felt hot, exciting that I couldn't separate them any further...I was forced to work harder to pleasure myself.

Trembling now, and frantic for release, I slid a finger inside and stroked myself some more, teasingly, relentlessly. At the same time I slid my other hand into my bra and caressed my nipple, squeezing and kneading as it swelled beneath my palm, then hardened into a knot of delicious sensation. Eyes closed, I pretended that it was the pirate who was fondling my bud so sweetly right now, that he was the one who was thrusting his fingers up into my pussy.

Quickly, the pleasure grew stronger, hotter, until my insides felt tied up in knots; and even as the dark-haired woman cried out, an orgasm crashed through me and left me gasping for breath. Eyes still closed, hunched over from the intense sensation, I rubbed my moist, open cleft slowly to draw every last little bit of pleasure from it, to draw out the ecstasy until finally, only a warm glow remained.

With a deep, yet quiet sigh, I dragged my panties up and allowed my dress to fall down. I leaned down to grab my camera and, as I straightened, I heard the pirate groan, the sound a long, drawn-out moan of pleasure and satisfaction. Intrigued, I stole a look through the opening. She was still straddling him, his hands supporting her beneath her bottom, but he was no longer thrusting into her. She was laying across him, looking exhausted.

Suddenly, she opened her eyes and saw me. She tensed and whispered something in his ear.

A rush of adrenaline flooded my veins.

I turned and ran, down the hallway, down the stairs, faster than I'd ever run before, my camera bouncing painfully against my chest. I kept running, even after I'd realized they weren't following me. I left the hotel, raced past the boat and kept going until I reached the tent. I saw Carlos pulling down the drive and hurried toward his car, hopping in before he even had a chance to stop. I knew the construction workers were staring at me, and even Carlos looked concerned.

I didn't care. I only knew I had to escape before they caught up with me.

Carlos stared at me with his eyebrows drawn together. "Everything okay, Miss?"

I gulped and managed a nod. "A peacock hiding inside the hotel scared me," I invented. "I'm fine."

He chuckled. "That old building is full of shadows. Just be careful, next time you go in there."

"I will." I settled back against the T-bird's seat and removed the camera strap from my neck.

"Did you get some good photos?" he asked.

I glanced thoughtfully at the camera. "I believe I did."

Carlos nodded happily. "Mr. Baxter will be pleased."

I said nothing in reply. I doubted Mr. Baxter would be pleased with photos of townies going at it in his newest hotel. But they pleased me, even though they also made me feel a strange mixture of shame and excitement.

I couldn't wait to get back to my hotel room and go through them.

CHAPTER FIVE

Carlos dropped me off at the hotel by dinner time. I hurried through the front door and into the lobby with a frown. I felt strange, out-of-sorts, altered in some way by what I'd witnessed, and even participated in. My heart still pounded in my chest and my breath came quickly, but even worse, I now had a restless yearning inside, a need I didn't want to acknowledge.

For the first time in my life, I was having trouble of thinking of anything but sex.

As I walked past the bar, I caught a glimpse of myself in a mirror and cringed: my hair was frizzy, with tendrils flying all over the place. Even worse, my face looked red. Sunburned.

I cast a harried glance over the male patrons at the bar and silently prayed that my 'date' wasn't there to see me. Natalie had been quite specific—I was to be at my best when I met him.

The bartender gave me a little smile and shrug, as if to say, what can I get you?

I forced my lips into an answering smile and kept going. I had two hours.

Natalie had said she'd send something up for me to wear. Once again, she was dressing me. The rest was my responsibility, though. I hadn't brought much makeup, so I ducked into a little shop off the lobby and bought a basic-brand lipstick, foundation, blush, and eyeliner. That done, I rushed up to my room, flung my camera onto the bed, and hopped into the shower. Groaning when I saw the ground-in dirt on the soles of my feet, I scrubbed the hell out of them, then washed my hair and loaded the conditioner on. A sense of panic was setting in as I finished my shower.

I had to look good. My best, in fact. But usually when I tried this hard to look good, I ended up looking too made-up, too phony. I blew a harassed breath out and ran over to the mini bar. I found a bottle of red wine, hastily popped it, poured myself a glass, and then set about blow-drying my hair.

Hair. Now that was a sore subject for me. I had the kind that didn't blow-dry very well. Light brown and shot with gold highlights, it hung half-way down my back and had a natural curl to it. Not only did blow-drying leave it frizzy, but it also took a year and a day to get it completely dry. I usually just let it air dry. Still, I didn't have that kind of time tonight. Wishing desperately for a diffuser, I nevertheless started the dryer and hit it with hot air.

Someone knocked on my hotel room door.

Shit.

I put the dryer down and raced over to the door. Opened it. A bellboy handed me a plastic-wrapped package. I fished in my wallet for a tip and thanked him. He left, and I opened the package.

My mouth fell open with shock.

The gown was floor-length. Deep blue. Made of a gauzy material, like chiffon. It had no straps and was close-fitting to the waistline. Then it belled out in gorgeous layers, ending just above my ankle.

I didn't think I'd ever seen anything quite as beautiful. It was a dress fit for a movie star. I checked the label: Emilio Pucci. I didn't recognize the name, but I could tell from the fabric and cut that the dress was expensive.

How in hell was I going to do this gown justice?

I went in to overdrive, styling my hair and using gobs of hair product. I pulled my hair back, let it hang naturally, then pulled it back again, thinking the second look more sophisticated. I put on makeup, took it off, and put it on again. Remembering Natalie's admonition, I put on some perfume I'd brought with me from Maine, a locally-made fragrance that smelled like the sea. I slipped into the dress and the high heel shoes that came with it, and paled when I saw how easily my breasts could pop out of the bodice. I took a few steps in the shoes and realized that my feet had never arched quite that high.

And yet, I felt sexy in a way that I never had before. And relaxed—the wine had seen to that. At five minutes before showtime, I took one final look in the mirror. My hair looked silky-smooth and hadn't the slightest bit of frizz, thanks to all that product. I'd wound it in a bun and pinned it to the back of my head, giving me that sophisticated air I'd been trying for. The sunburn had faded, and now my skin simply glowed. I'd used coral-colored lipstick and a touch of blush; and highlighted my blue eyes with champagne-colored eye shadow.

And the dress...well, it fit like a glove, hugging my breasts and waist before belling out around my legs. For once, I didn't mind my D-cups; this kind of dress required a decent amount of cleavage to keep it up. I adjusted the straps on my black velvet high heels, then grabbed my makeup bag, which I'd converted into an evening bag. Seconds later, I was out the door and descending to the lobby via an elevator.

The elevator opened near the Barcelona's restaurant. While the front portion of the hotel had resembled a rich man's study, this part had more in common with a bird of paradise: rich turquoise walls, gold wall sconces topped with little white shades, white trim, and bouquets of brilliant red and orange flowers everywhere.

I strode into this wild luxury, feeling transformed into bird of paradise myself, with my deep blue, form-fitting gown and high heels. Heads turned as I sauntered toward the bar: women whispered behind their hands, and men observed me with a smile or narrowed eyes. After they checked me out, they went back to their conversations. I had a feeling that this was the kind of place where appearances mattered above all else.

I surveyed the room. A man in a white tuxedo was playing piano pushed off to the side, and women dressed in slinky black numbers were laughing and flirting with middle-aged men who sat at the bar. The women looked a lot younger than the men. Wives, girlfriends, escorts? I wondered, then sidled up to the bar.

Play it again, Sam, I debating saying to the piano player.

The waitresses, all of them with their hair held up by multi-colored gauze wraps, shook cocktail shakers and made pina coladas, their stacked gold bracelets jingling against their tanned skin. One of them asked me what I wanted. I requested a strawberry daiquiri, and she went to work on it.

I turned my attention to the men once more and surveyed each of them in turn. I was searching for a loner. Where was this date Natalie had stuck me with?

All at once, I felt warm air fanning across my neck. My heart sped up. I turned around. Caught my breath.

It was him. The pirate, the man from Beau Paradis. Up close, his eyes were a deep blue, like the deepest waters of a forest pool. At the moment, they were coolly studying me.

"The dress fits," he observed.

I forced a smile, tried to look unconcerned, and smoothed my hair down. "You're the investor who was supposed to meet Natalie Shelby here tonight?"

"You're obviously her replacement." He searched my face, as if looking for something. "Blue looks good on you. I wasn't sure if it would fit."

I gulped. Felt oddly vulnerable, all at once. "You sent this dress up to my room?"

For the first time, he smiled, drawing my attention to his full lower lip. "Do you like it?"

"Yes..."

He nodded arrogantly. "Good. She asked me to pick something out for you. She said you came down here unprepared for anything but a snowstorm."

My cheeks started heating up. "But how did you know my size?"

"I saw you come in a few hours ago." His focus slipped lower, assessing my full breasts and narrow waist; then returned to my face. "You'll keep it, of course."

His gaze left my skin feeling hot. Exposed. I

wanted to hide my breasts with my hands. Traitorously, my nipples hardened. "I'm not sure I should be accepting a dress from a man I don't know...but thanks anyway."

He lifted one arched eyebrow. "My name's Jon. Jon Baxter."

I stared at him, dumbfounded. Jon Baxter? The Jon Baxter, owner of the company I now worked for? "Uh..."

His lips quirked in a half-smile.

I gulped, tried not to speak too quickly as I replied. "Mr. Baxter! I'm sorry, Natalie told me you were an investor. I'm new to the company, but that's no excuse, I should have recognized you—"

He cut me off. "I own the hotel, so I am an investor. You are Demeter O'Reilly, right? Nat's new assistant?"

I gulped and nodded. "Yes, that's me."

"I'm glad to hear that," he murmured. "I'd really feel like a fool if you weren't."

I laughed nervously. My head was spinning. Natalie had lined up a 'date' with Jon Baxter? Why the hell hadn't she told me? I silently recalled the things she'd warned me about: he's worth a lot of money, but he's smart, and used to getting what he wants. But he was also my ultimate boss. "I'm really sorry, Mr. Baxter. I feel like a fool. Natalie didn't mention who I would be meeting—"

"Call me Jon," he cut in. "Don't feel bad. Nat's a whirlwind. The fact that she didn't tell you who I was doesn't surprise me. She has so much going on, she can't even keep her own name straight."

My heart was beating out a quick, painful rhythm in my chest as I silently admitted that if I'd known I'd be meeting Jon Baxter, by myself, for a date, I probably would have holed up in my hotel room and never come out.

"I usually go by the nickname Demmie," I managed.

He smiled and dipped his head lower, toward my neck, just for an instant. I had the impression that he wanted to smell my perfume.

A waitress with long, dark hair joined us and handed me my daiquiri. She gave Jon the once-over and then offered him a saucy smile. "Drink?"

He shook his head. "Maybe later."

Pouting, she moved off.

I took a sip of my daiquiri, a big one.

"I heard you were over at Beau Paradis this afternoon," he said. "What did you think?"

Immediately I remembered his gorgeous naked ass, and how he'd so masterfully drilled that dark-haired woman. "It's beautiful," I choked out. "I can only imagine what it will look like when the construction teams finish with it."

"Nat's driver told me that something frightened you while you were in the hotel. A peacock, I think you said."

I felt my cheeks grow hotter. "It was hiding in the shadows. It just...jumped out at me."

His smile widened, became edged with mockery. "No doubt it wasn't expecting to see you in there."

"I'm sure I surprised it," I agreed faintly.

"Did you manage to take any photos of it? I'd love to see them."

I took another big gulp of my daiquiri. "No photos of any peacocks, but lots of the interior. Natalie's asked me to think of a branding campaign for the hotel."

"And did you find your visit inspiring?"

"More so than you'd ever believe," I replied, the words sounding strangled to my ears.

He laughed aloud.

Completely embarrassed, I looked down at the floor. After I'd gathered my courage, I glanced up, and saw he was watching me.

"Let's go to dinner," he said, and nodded toward the double-doors at the far end of the lobby. "We'll walk. I want to get to know you...especially since we'll be spending the next several days together."

I stumbled. He quickly grasped my arm and steadied me.

"The next several days?" I asked faintly.

"Didn't Nat tell you?" He quirked an eyebrow. "I'm going to keep an eye on you until she gets back."

I nodded, as if the idea of Natalie Selby giving orders to one of the company's owners wasn't strange at all. "I think she's going to be fun to work for."

"Oh, she's fun, all right," he agreed.

I continued to follow him through the lobby. Discreetly I eyed his tall, powerful form; his superbly tailored suit, his tawny hair, and reminded myself several times over that he was my boss. I saw him doing the same thing: sizing up my breasts, my legs, my face. I swallowed hard and, my stomach fluttering, tried not to think of that naked ass of his.

The way he was looking at me made me feel tingly. Uncomfortable, even, in a way I didn't know how to explain, even to myself. I dared to give him a chastising glance, and his lips curled provocatively before he checked me out again, purposefully, his gaze lingering—as if he wanted me to know that he'd look whenever he wanted, and had no intention of asking for my permission. The idea made me feel even more awkward. I quickly turned away and tripped on my high heels. Once again, he steadied me with a firm hand on my elbow. Then, smiling slightly, he released me.

As before, people watched us as we strolled toward the lobby exit. I sensed the stares of men lingering on me—they wanted to know what made me so special, that a man like Jon Baxter would want to walk with me. The truth was, nothing made me special. Somehow, I'd just gotten lucky. I'd won the job lottery. And the date lottery.

Lucky me.

My stomach continued doing flips. My heart still thumped out a hard rhythm in my chest. I knew I had to calm down soon, or pass out. Deliberately, slowly, I took several deep breaths and made sure not to glance at him. By the time we reached the doors, I could breathe again, though I knew I was blushing furiously—my cheeks were on fire.

We walked through the doors and out onto the sidewalk. Almost immediately I noticed a big, meaty-looking goon pause several feet behind us. "Your bodyguard?" I asked, as we stopped outside the doors.

He nodded.

"You need bodyguards around all the time?"

"I had someone rush me with a gun once. A crazy person who didn't like how B3 was buying up hotels in France. He was arrested, committed. I don't want to take the chance of getting shot again."

My eyes widened. Suddenly he seemed as exotic as a panther sauntering down Main Street. "Well, I'm glad you didn't get shot."

"I did get shot. It was a flesh wound. It healed quickly."

We turned right, headed south down Ocean Drive. I wobbled a little in my heels. "Oh."

The goon followed us. I also noticed a limousine cruising along several feet behind us. "A bodyguard must get you noticed a lot." As I said this, I watched a couple gawk at us as they passed us by on the opposite side of the street.

"People look. So what?"

"I don't think I'd like that, being constantly on display."

He slowed down, stopped, stared at me with narrowed eyes. "Do you want to take my car? Or should we take a bus?"

I smiled. "You'd take a bus?"

"Why not?"

My smile fled. I fidgeted a little. "I'm fine walking."

"Whatever you want." He nudged me with his shoulder, and I caught a clean male scent, something like baby shampoo and soap.

My heart started to beat faster. I glanced at him surreptitiously. He was so damned hot! I wondered how I was going to spend the next several days with him, when every time he got within five feet of me, I wanted to jump up, wrap my legs around his waist and ride him like the woman in Beau Paradis had.

We started walking again. He kept close to me, but didn't touch me. He didn't need to touch me. His eyes were gleaming with male appreciation that I couldn't fail to recognize. Clearly Mr. Baxter liked women. I was his next target, I supposed—the newly hired assistant. What had Natalie said? That he was smart, and gets what he wants. To be careful.

It was going to be hard to be careful around that.

We continued down Ocean Drive, past palm trees lit from beneath with orange spotlights, their trunks strung with glowing strands of lights. The buildings—art deco hotels, condominiums, boutiques—were mostly painted white, and lit with garish colors like magenta, purple, and yellow. I felt like I'd somehow stumbled into the Land of Oz.

It was growing dark and clouds rustled across the sky, bringing a cool breeze with them. I was re-thinking his car offer when we turned down a wide alley with bright, multi-colored lights strung from one side of the block to the other. Music played up ahead, a lively salsa melody, and the buildings on either side blocked the breeze. As we walked through this enchanted corridor, he reached up and pulled my hair from the bun I'd wound it in. Bobby pins fell to the cobblestone street.

He stroked my hair a little and smiled. "I like it better down."

I swallowed at the air of command about him, at the sheer arrogance of his gesture. Who was he, to decide how I should wear my hair? But his manner was so authoritative, I didn't dare complain, and my heart sped up once again at the way his eyes gleamed at me. Suddenly I was glad I had pleased him--and with so little effort, too. I slanted a little smile his way to show him that I didn't mind his boldness, and a glint of satisfaction entered his gaze.

We walked down the alley and then made a right onto a street that buzzed with activity. He seemed to have brought me to a street party with a Latin flavor.

Tourists and locals alike crowded the sidewalks and cobblestone streets and wandered around, eating, dancing, and playing carnival-like games of chance. A street vendor pushed a food cart that offered corn dogs and funnel cakes. Multi-color streamers hung down from wire stretched across the street, from building to building, and a little boy tended white ducks that waddled around a little penned-in area. Flowers, tropical ones, sprawled across the sidewalk and covered every hue in the rainbow. And in the corner, a band played salsa music with a catchy beat, inspiring couples to dance in the middle of the street.

I couldn't help but notice that he and I were dressed a lot more formally than everyone else around us. I wondered why he'd bought me this elegant evening gown if he'd planned to take me to a street party.

"Do you know how to salsa?" he asked.

I shook my head no. "Salsa isn't something we do up in Maine."

"What do you do up in Maine...for fun, that is?"

"Head down to the local bar and have a beer," I suggested, though I didn't typically hang around bars. The truth was, I'd never had much fun back home. At least not like I was having here.

"Now, why do I get the feeling you aren't a beer drinker?"

"I don't drink much of anything," I admitted. "Except water."

"And milk?" he teased.

I shrugged.

"Tonight, that's going to change," he promised, and grasped my arm. His grip like steel, steered me down another street with a torch-lit building at the end of it. "Don't worry, Demmie. I'll take care of you."

Suddenly we were feeling way too intimate. "Thanks, Mr. Baxter," I replied, deliberately using his last name.

"It's Jon," he reminded me.

I managed a nod in reply.

We continued on, past a vendor selling colorfully-hued silken scarves. I exclaimed over one that had a pattern of cornflowers on it, their blue petals contrasting with bright green leaves and yellow centers; and he promptly bought it for me and wound it around my shoulders.

I blushed and thanked him.

Surrounded by the sweet scents of flowers and funnel cakes, we headed toward the building with two torches on either side of the entrance. As we drew close, I noticed that both men and women waiting to get into the restaurant were dressed like us, and I realized that this building had always been our true destination.

"So...this is the restaurant you wanted to take me to?" I asked, as we approached the entrance.

"You'll enjoy it. It's different. It's Miami." He held my arm as we stopped in front of the hostess, who smiled widely when she saw who it was.

"Mr. Baxter," the woman said, "how wonderful to see you again. Welcome. How are you?" She grabbed my hand as a courtesy, and Jon placed his hand on the small of my back. Up ahead, on the landing, several parrots hopped around in the most eye-popping display of tropical flowers I'd ever seen.

We climbed the stairs toward the parrots, with the hostess smiling and chit-chatting with us the whole time. She moved slowly, gracefully, and when we reached the landing, she stopped to pet one of the birds, her purple shawl draping seductively from her arms.

The parrot squawked in what seemed like a desperate attempt to speak. I could have sworn it said be careful.

"What did it say?" I asked

"Mia cara," she answered softly. "Darling mine. It's Italian."

I laughed a little, and stroked the parrot a few times more, hoping it would speak again. But then the hostess touched my arm, and I looked behind me.

Jon had disappeared.

She gestured toward another set of stairs beneath an arch. This set descended downward. As I strolled through the arch, I saw that the restaurant was situated in what looked like a grotto, with stone columns, ferns growing from the walls and waterfalls flowing freely from the ceiling. Tables were situated between the columns, all of them a discreet distance each other, and flowers overflowed from urns placed strategically around the room.

All of the tables were filled. Couples of every shape and size were enjoying wine, champagne, and meals served with silver flatware on white porcelain. All of the diners appeared to have one thing in common: money. Expensive-looking, colorful dresses; finely tailored black tuxedos, diamond jewelry, beautiful tanned faces—this was clearly a playground for the wealthy.

The waitresses wore silk saris, and the waiters had on gauzy linen pants and shirts. They all looked fit, in shape, like the diners themselves; and had on various types of gold jewelry. One of the waiters moved to my side as I reached the bottom of the stairs, and guided me toward a table in the corner, where Jon sat, watching me. Jon, I saw, had a slender cigar between his fingers. While waiting for me, he'd lit it. A tendril of smoke drifted from its end.

The waiter pulled the chair out and helped me to sit down. Then he put a napkin across my legs, poured water into my glass, filled my crystal flute with champagne, bowed, and left us.

Jon and I faced each other across the table. Candles set in a grouping between us flickered, washing everything with a golden haze. Tropical flowers perfumed the air around us with a pleasing scent. Pink champagne bubbled invitingly in my glass. The atmosphere was subtly, yet undeniably, erotic. A combination of anticipation and panic filled me.

He sat back, his cigar in hand, the silver band he wore on his index finger glistening beneath the lights. He took in my thick, shiny hair; that scarf that he'd bought me, which now draped around my naked shoulders, and the luxurious low-cut navy gown. "I like watching you walk. You move gracefully."

I quirked an eyebrow, thinking this a bald-faced lie. I was a Maine bumpkin, an ugly duckling—not the graceful swan he was painting me as. But I kept the thought to myself. I didn't think I'd impress him by disagreeing with him and disparaging myself.

He set the cigar aside and lifted his champagne glass. "A toast—to us."

"To us?"

"To a long and productive working relationship," he amended.

I picked up my glass, lifted it. "To us." I sipped the bubbles. They tasted sweet, but also tart, and they fizzed against my tongue as they went down.

"Do you like it?" he asked.

"It's wonderful." The champagne simmered in my stomach with a gentle warmth.

"If you're going to drink champagne, this is the one." He sipped his again.

I picked up the bottle with my free hand and studied the label. "Krug, 1998. Clos d'Ambonnay." Shrugging, I put it down. "I'm sure you've spoiled champagne for me forever. Nothing else will ever be as good."

He studied me some more, and his mouth lifted at the corners. "Is this your first taste of champagne?"

I felt that annoying blush heat up my cheeks again. Unwillingly, I nodded.

He picked up his cigar, took a puff. "Someday, you'll be able to tell your grandchildren that you had your first taste of champagne in old converted servants' quarters."

"That's what this restaurant used to be?"

He nodded. "It was slave quarters before that."

I looked around, shuddered a little. "It's very pretty, now."

"If I'd have known you'd never tasted champagne before, I would have brought you to a champagne bar. You could have picked from a hundred different kinds of bubbly there." He took another puff on his cigar and cocked his head. Looked thoughtful. "I'm surprised no one mentioned that."

"Surprised?" I shook my head. "I don't understand."

"I didn't approve your hire until we'd done a

background check," he told me. "Your mom had a lot of things to say, but she never mentioned the champagne."

"My mom?"

"My people called her as part of the check. I hope you don't mind."

I frowned. I felt as though he'd just stripped the dress off of me and left me naked. "What else did she say?"

"Just that you loved photography, and that you'd be a hard worker, both loyal and devoted."

"Well, I'm glad I passed your background check."

"She also told me about your dad."

I sucked in a breath looked down at my hands. He'd touched a raw nerve. It hurt.

Silence stretched between us for an instant. I sensed him studying me. Then he sat back. "Your mom's very nice. She mentioned that you hadn't many boyfriends."

Relieved to not have to make up excuses about my father, I slumped a little. "I guess I was always too involved with school, photography." I paused, swallowed. "What about you?"

He smiled. "Do I have a boyfriend?"

I choked, blushed a little more. Glanced at the silver ring he wore on the index finger of his right hand. "No, no, of course not. Are you married? Do you have a family?"

He watched me from beneath heavy-lidded eyes, his expression suddenly hidden. "I'm not marrying material."

I considered his answer. At first, delight filled me. He wasn't married! But then, I understood from the inflection in his voice that despite his single status, he was still unavailable.

"That's fine with me. I'm not marrying material, either," I agreed.

"Hmmm. No boyfriends, and you're not marrying material. You don't seem too interested in matters of the heart."

"Neither do you."

"Touché." He glanced at his cigar. "You don't mind the cigar, do you?"

I shook my head no and gulped my champagne.

After a moment, he held the cigar out toward me, glowing end pointed away. "Want to try it?"

I heard the subtle challenge in his tone and took the cigar from him. Trying to look as cool and sophisticated as possible, I lifted the cigar to my lips and slipped it between them. It felt warm and slightly moist. All at once, I couldn't stop thinking about the fact that he'd just held the same cigar between his lips.

I drew air in through the cigar, and smoke flooded my mouth. I pretended like I enjoyed it, but then let out a little cough. My eyes watered. I grabbed the champagne with my free hand and took a sip.

He laughed and took the cigar from me. "Another first, right?"

"I don't smoke," I said.

"You haven't experienced much," he mused.

I nodded hesitantly. He made me feel so off-kilter, so unsure. I'd never met a man like him before...and my heart had never raced before as it was tonight.

"Did you know that happiness comes from experiences, not things?" he continued. "If you truly want to be happy, you need to allow yourself to experience, to see what you like."

"This is your philosophy on how to get the most out of life?"

"It is."

"Well," I noted thoughtfully, "I experienced champagne tonight, and I liked it."

He took another puff on his cigar, and then stubbed it out. "You're all potential, Demmie. You're 'experience' waiting to happen."

"I'm ready to experience whatever you throw at me," I replied, and sat there, amazed that such bold words had found their way out of my mouth.

Then he smiled, and I knew I'd pleased him. A warm glow of satisfaction wound through me; but at the same time, I felt a little ridiculous. This work date with Mr. Baxter had been like riding a rollercoaster. He became annoyed, and I wanted to drop through the floor. He praised me, and I felt light as a feather. I had to get control of myself.

I picked up my champagne glass and finished off the rest of it. Seconds later, a waiter was at my side, refilling my glass. I took another sip. "So tell me, what experience have you had, that has changed you the most?"

"Hmmm." He looked down at his plate, considered. After a moment, he glanced back up at me. "There was a woman in my life once. She was young, and very beautiful. I was even younger."

He paused, and I could see he was thinking. Searching his memory. "How young were you?" I asked.

"About thirteen years old," he replied.

I swallowed. "Who was she?"

"My nanny, at first. When I was much younger. By the time I was thirteen, she'd become my tutor--

for mathematics, English, that kind of thing. She was very smart, and accomplished in many ways."

"So what happened?"

"I was kind of a punk, I guess. I spent most of my time rebelling." He smiled a little. "Her room was directly below mine, and sometimes I could hear her having sex with someone. Moaning, and sighs, and groans of pleasure. It drove me insane, thinking of some other man between my nanny's thighs. So one night, I took my camera, and hid in her room. In her closet."

I swallowed, hard, at his mention of sex and camera.

He began to toy with his fork. "A man came in. My father, in fact. He made love to her, and I took photos of them. And the next day, I showed her the photos. I told her that I was also going to show them to my mother."

"Oh, God," I breathed.

"Yes, I know," he agreed. "I really had a set of balls on me, hiding in there and photographing them while they were fucking."

I froze. He'd seen me in the hotel, I thought wildly. And now he was having fun with me.

"Anyway, the moment she saw those photos, she ripped the camera out of my hands and threw it across the room," he continued. "She yanked my pants down, turned me over her knee, and spanked me until I begged for mercy."

I gave him a surprised look, but inside, my pulse was pounding.

"And once she felt I had begged enough, she turned me over and set me on the bed. And then she got down between my legs. She took my cock into her mouth and worked my balls with her hand until I lost control and exploded into her mouth." He paused, looked me directly in the eyes. "It was my very first blow job. And it was once hell of an experience."

Suddenly I felt hot, tingly. I fought the urge to fan myself. "So you, ah, shared her with your father?"

"My father never fucked her again. I don't know why—maybe she told him what had happened. Whatever the case, we were an item from that day forward."

"For how long?"

"A few years. Eventually my father paid her off. Later on, she got married. We still keep in touch."

I nodded, my expression neutral, though inside, I felt tight, wound-up.

Moments later, the waiters brought out a salad for each of us. That ended the discussion. From there, we chit-chatted as we ate: first the salad, then appetizers made of various kinds of seafood, followed by an entrée of tiger prawns, grilled vegetables and jasmine rice. Throughout it all, we continued drinking champagne, until they brought out delicate little ice cream cakes. At that point we switched to port, which was also a first for me.

I was sipping the rich red liquid and thinking how easy it would be, to get used to a life like this, when John sat back and regarded me from beneath heavy eyelids. He looked unconcerned, almost sleepy; and yet I could sense the piercing intellect behind his lazy exterior.

"Tell me about an experience that changed your life," he demanded.

I nodded and thought about it, but everything that

occurred to me seemed so incredibly foolish or depressing compared to his story, that my only answer was a shrug. What could I tell him—about the day I received my first puppy? The day my father passed away?

"Tell me," he urged.

I smiled uneasily. "The day I won B3's photography contest, my life changed forever. It led me here, to Miami, and to this new job. It's really very exciting."

He shook his head. "That's not what I'm looking for. I want to know about an experience that rocked you deep inside. Something that changed your view of the world forever."

He stared at me with those blue eyes of his, eyes that saw everything, and abruptly I couldn't think. I could only stare back, my stomach fluttering wildly. Witnessing him having sex with that woman had changed me in ways I'd never dreamed of. But how could I tell him that?

"You're afraid to tell me, aren't you?"

I couldn't have spoken if I wanted to. My lips didn't want to speak. An image of him naked, and settling the waitress down onto his hard cock, filled my head. Dumbly I shook my head yes.

"All right, then," he said. "How about we talk about someone else."

"Someone else? Who?"

He nodded toward a dark-haired woman who was dining with two blonde guys. "Her."

I could only see her profile, but she looked familiar, somehow. Her two friends looked like beach bums—I didn't recognize them at all. "I don't think I know her."

"You don't need to. What are your impressions about her?"

Glad to be let off the hook, I glanced discreetly at the woman. "She looks like she's in her mid-thirties. She's wealthy, obviously." I eyed the slightly sour twist to her mouth, the only negative feature on her otherwise beautiful face, and added, "She's unhappy, too."

"Why is she unhappy?"

"Because the man she loves doesn't want to be with her," I invented on the spot, and smiled. So now we were playing games.

"Why doesn't he want her?" he asked.

I thought for a moment. "He has someone else, someone wealthier and more beautiful."

He smiled approvingly. "You have a good imagination."

"She's wanted him forever, but she's not good enough for him."

"That's a shame. How does she know she loves him?"

I returned his gaze, mesmerized by the warmth in his dark, sleepy-looking eyes. "Because of the way he makes her feel."

"How does he make her feel?"

"Breathless." I drew in a quick breath. "He makes her heart pound."

He grabbed my hand, turned my palm up, and traced the lines crossing my palm. "What would make her lose control?"

My palm burned where he touched me. Suddenly feeling overwhelmed, I turned away, made a big deal of studying her. At that very moment, she turned to face me.

Immediately I recognized her as the woman he'd been screwing at Beau Paradis.

My internal temperature plummeted several degrees. This couldn't be by chance, I thought frantically. "I don't know what would make her lose control," I stuttered, wanting the game over.

But clearly he wasn't going to let go so easily.

"Make something up," he suggested. "Just like you've been doing."

Several seconds passed, during which I frantically tried to come up with something. "The man that she loves...he could take her to Beau Paradis," I finally whispered, unable to think of anything but the truth.

"Continue," he urged.

I swallowed. "He would kiss her and make love to her there." Unable to meet his gaze any longer, I looked down at my hand, which he still held within his much larger one.

"How would he make love to her?" he murmured, his voice a deep, husky rasp. "What would he do?"

"I don't know. I don't want to think about it."

His fingers curled around mine. "Tell me."

I looked up then, and silently pleaded with him to stop asking me these questions, to let me go.

"Imagine he does want her, and he's taken her to Beau Paradis to have sex with her." He traced his finger delicately across my palm. "You're there now, watching them. Tell me what you see."

"Well," I murmured in a small voice, "he's kissing her—"

"Does she have clothes on?"

"A dress only. A sari."

"Something he could easily take off her. Very nice," he purred. "And him, is he dressed?"

"He's naked." I paused, fanned myself. I knew I must have looked foolish, but my cheeks were flaming hot. I was actually starting to feel dizzy. "It's hot in here."

He smiled. "Very." He turned my hand over, started tracing my knuckles with a feathery touch. "Are they standing under a broken pipe, and letting the water wash over them?

I nodded, felt my face burning. "They are."

"And he touches her very gently, because she isn't used to him. She hasn't had a lot of men."

"No, she hasn't," I agreed. "But he doesn't touch her gently. He takes her...in a forceful way."

"Hmmm. Why does he do that?" Those hooded, seductive eyes of his gazed darkly at me over the top of his champagne glass and told me he couldn't look away from me, that I had charmed him, just as he'd fascinated me. I didn't think I'd ever seen such a look in a man's eyes before, especially directed at me. Then again, I realized now that until Jon, I had known only boys—

"Why, Demmie? Why does he take her so savagely?"

"I don't know," I murmured.

"I think you do," he replied. "I think you know why, but you're afraid to tell me."

"I'm not afraid." My heart thumping hard, I met his gaze directly.

Without warning, he pushed back from the table and stood.

I froze. My heart thumped hard. Somehow, I reached up and grabbed his arm. "Wait. Don't go. I'll tell you," I breathed. "He possesses her that way because...that's what she wants." I wondered if he could see my pulse beating in my neck.

"She likes to...surrender."

I saw the teasing glint in his eyes, and my frustration boiled over. I released his arm. "Yes, she surrenders, and more! She'll do anything to be with him, in fact. He makes her realize what she's always been missing." I stole a glance at the dark-haired woman, who had unknowingly become the centerpiece of my fantastic story.

His huge fingers curled possessively around mine, clasping them firmly, his thumb gently scratching the inside of my palm. "Come with me. I want to show you something."

We stood up from the table. He clasped my arm and led me through the restaurant, and up the stairs. Once we reached the landing with the tropical flowers and parrots, I expected to turn left, toward the exit. Instead, he guided me down a hallway to the right, and through an arched doorway that led to a large patio area.

Once through the doorway, we paused, and I tried to take it all in.

The area stretched far, far back...all the way to the beach; and appeared to be one of the sexiest, most intimate clubs I'd ever set eyes on. Couples lounged on white pillows atop rattan sofas and chairs. Others ordered drinks at bars, or accepted drinks from waitresses who roamed through the sand in bikinis, with trays balanced on their arms. Latin-style instrumental music filtered through unseen speakers, and beneath it, I heard the distant sound of waves crashing against the shore.

Torches were set in the sand, or attached to poles, in various places. They provided the only illumination on the patio, creating more shadows than light and allowing the couples not only intimacy, but also anonymity. I couldn't see anyone's features--I just had a general sense of men and women close together, laughing and drinking.

A stone path wound its way through the patio area and toward the beach. Jon led me down the path, where the sofas and chairs gave way to white-draped beds and cabanas situated right in the sand. My steps slowed as I saw, on one of the beds, a naked couple—the man was on top, nestled between the woman's legs—

I drew in a sharp breath and turned away.

Jon leaned toward me. "Relax," he said.

"How can I relax?" I muttered. "That couple is having sex right in front of everyone. Where I come from, that's called public indecency."

"You're not in Kansas anymore, Dorothy," he said with a little smile. "Things are different here. And we're not in public, by the way. We're in a club."

"A sex club?"

He didn't answer. Rather, he pulled me past the couple, further down the stone path to a clearing. The clearing contained a dance floor with a few tables on either side of it. On the far end, a band was setting up. A couple of the musicians were playing off-cue, presumably to check that their instruments were tuned. A riff of bongo-playing and trumpet blasts filled the air, and more couples moved toward the dance floor.

A brief silence ensued as the musicians stopped testing their instruments, and then started to play. Their melody was a strange one—languid, sultry, but with an edge; seductive yet full of energy. As the bongos played harder and quicker, one of the waitresses put her tray down and began to dance, her movements sinuous, sexy.

Jon guided me back a little, out of the way of the waitress, but where I'd still have a good view of the dance floor. Quietly he moved behind me. I couldn't see him, but I didn't need to. I felt him standing there, warm and big and solid.

I watched as the waitress reached her arms to the sky, smiling joyously, her breasts swaying as she gyrated to the music. Her blatantly erotic about her movements seemed, at least to me, at odds with the look of devout bliss on her face, and I wondered what kind of sex club this was: The Church of Sacred Sex? The message seemed to be that sex was a religious experience.

I smiled, amused and shocked at the same time.

Moments later, she melted back into the crowd, and another waitress took her place. The second waitress moved just as sinuously as the first, gyrating her hips in a way that made me think of the couple having sex on the bed. Then, all around her, others began to dance, sensuously, their movements abandoned, their faces lit with enjoyment.

I gulped. I felt really uncomfortable. Back home, the joys of sex didn't typically come up in casual conversation and we certainly didn't act it out. It's not that the people in my town disliked sex--they just didn't talk about it or celebrate it so openly. But this...this was a festival of sex, an orgy, despite the fact that most people on the dance floor were dressed. And somehow, watching it with Jon behind me made me squirm even more.

And yet, I wasn't immune to what I was seeing. I

felt moisture slicking the inside of my thighs, and embarrassment shot through me. My conscience told me to leave right away, that it wasn't proper for me to be watching this. But at the same time, an intense yearning—a painful tension buried deep inside me—kept me rooted to the spot.

I stared, wide-eyed, as a third waitress replaced the second. This latest one had a skin-tight lace evening gown. Again, she danced in a way to tempt, to seduce...and then a man dressed in a tuxedo separated from the audience to dance with her. He appeared very Latin, and very handsome, and my breath caught in my throat at the way he looked at her.

Caught up in their sensuality, I moved back a little. I was hoping to nudge against Jon. But I felt nothing. I turned to look, and saw that he was talking to that dark-haired woman in the restaurant, the one he'd been intimate with in Beau Paradis.

I frowned. I had no right to feel jealous. And yet...my gut soured at the sight.

I turned back to the dance floor. Watched. Felt even more uncomfortable than before. The couple was still dancing. Back and forth they moved, giving and taking, and then he was holding her, moving her, guiding her. He had his hands on her exposed skin, and he was stroking, caressing... They looked like were having sex just as surely as the horizontal couple on the bed.

The tension inside me tightened.

All of a sudden, the dancing couple whirled toward a chair someone had set upon the dance floor. When they reached it, the woman sat down and spread her thighs wide apart. The man gracefully moved into position between her legs and began to push against her, oblivious to the fact that they both had clothes on. The woman writhed in ecstasy as the man threw his head back, grabbed her thighs, and thrust in time with the music.

I crossed my arms over my breasts. Astonishment and embarrassment twisted through me, demanding that I leave before it went any further. At the same time, the tension inside me centered between my thighs and tightened deliciously. My nipples hardened and started to ache. I wanted to be the woman on the chair, with Jon as the man. I desperately wanted to feel him inside me—

Someone moved the scarf around my shoulders aside. Warm lips suddenly pressed against my neck.

I stopped breathing, electrified by the sensation. My pulse pounded. Moisture gushed between my thighs. I leaned backwards into him, stretched my neck to give him better access, and closed my eyes.

"Mmmm," I whispered.

He pressed several more kisses up and down my neck, his lips firm, silky, demanding.

I moaned and turned slightly, not sure what I was going to say, only knowing that I needed him desperately---

I found myself looking into the dark brown eyes of a man I didn't know. A playful glint lit them. "You're very beautiful," he murmured.

I drew in a sharp breath, took a stumbling step backward. The heat inside me went instantly cold.

He quirked an eyebrow. He was very good-looking, I saw, with black hair and a muscular build.

I stared at him, aghast, my voice failing me. "I...I..."

He leaned forward to kiss my neck again, but

before his lips could connect, I spun away.

Obeying some primal instinct, I pulled up my dress hem and ran, weaving through the couples and finding the stone path; hurrying up the stone path and into the building, then out into the alley. As I hit the cobblestones in the alley, I lost one of my shoes, but I kept going, until I reached the street. There, I hailed a taxi. It wasn't until I was tucked safely into the taxi's rear seat, and had given the driver the name of my hotel, that the tears came.

I wasn't even sure why I was crying. Maybe it was because the sex club had been a revelation of sorts. Revelations were typically scary things, because they threatened to change the way you lived. Or maybe the tears came from a feeling of abandonment. Jon had abandoned me, after all. He'd left me to chat up his lover. Clearly there wasn't anything special between us—we were just boss and employee.

But deep inside, I knew the true reason why I'd run away and was now crying. I was lusting after a man I couldn't have, and it felt dangerous to me. He hadn't fucked me yet, but I desperately wanted to earn that privilege, and I wasn't used to being held hostage by my own out-of-control desire.

Throughout my life, I'd always known exactly what I'd wanted. I'd always gone after it. Until I'd met Jon, building a career as a photographer had seemed the most important, sensible thing I could do. But now, for the first time, I couldn't see the way ahead. I didn't know what the future would, or should hold for me.

I wasn't sure if I'd ever been more scared in my entire life.

CHAPTER SIX

Insistent knocking on my door woke me up the next morning. I'd been dreaming about something I couldn't remember, but it had left me restless. And so, when I opened my eyes, I felt like I hadn't slept at all, and I considered throwing something at the door, to get the person on the other side to stop banging.

"Housekeeping," a woman announced from the hallway.

I groaned and pushed my head beneath the pillow.

"Should I let her in?" a male voice asked in silky tones.

My heart gave a wild thump. Slowly, I sat up and turned toward the voice.

Jon was sitting there, his big body folded into a chair by the desk. He wore a pair of jeans and T-shirt, the clothes clinging to his tall, well-muscled form; and his thick hair looked slightly tousled. He smiled, his full mouth curving, pink, lower lip taut; and watched me from beneath heavy drooping eyelids that hid the expression in his eyes.

Behind him, bouquets of roses, lilies, freesia, and other tropical flowers I couldn't name decorated the bureau, the desk, and the television stand. All at once, I smelled their almost overpowering fragrance.

My gaze cut to the desk near the chair where he

sat. My camera was sitting atop the desk. Panic sliced through me. My God—if he saw those pictures--

"Housekeeping!" The doorknob began to turn.

He was up in a flash and at the door, blocking the woman from coming in. "Later," he told her. He shut the door and locked it. Then, he returned to his seat by the desk, his expression unapologetic.

I pulled the sheets up to my shoulders and frowned. "How did you get in here?"

"Why did you run away last night?" he asked.

"Who did you bribe? The maid? The concierge?"

He smiled and picked up something from the floor. He held it up for me to see.

My high-heeled shoe. The one I'd lost in my mad dash from the sex club.

"You lost this, Cinderella," he informed me, and set the shoe back on the floor. His gaze roved over what he could see of my Lanz of Salzburg cotton nightgown. "Cute pajamas."

I lifted my chin. He made me feel so vulnerable. "Why are you here?"

"You ran away from me last night," he said. "That doesn't happen very often. I want to know why."

A hundred words, a hundred explanations crowded my lips at once: the champagne had gone to my head, the wild lifestyle that he seemed to take for granted had shocked me. All of them seemed lame, though. And of course, I couldn't tell him the truth: that he seemed to be shaping up as the experience that would change my entire life—whether he wanted to or not—and that this understanding had frightened me. I looked away from him, acutely aware of the sexuality he exuded from every pore. "I never thanked you for the dinner. The dress. Everything. Thank you."

"You're welcome," he said.

A few moments passed. He waited. I had a sense that he'd wait all day if he had to.

"Somebody kissed my neck at the club," I revealed, feeling that I had to say something. "A man I didn't know."

He quirked a disbelieving eyebrow. "A stolen kiss made you run away?"

I crossed my arms over my chest and scowled. "I'm not used to this...this life of yours. Where I come from, people are expected to act modestly. Sensibly. So that's how I've always behaved—modestly, and sensibly. But last night was anything but modest and sensible. Besides that, my family never had a lot of money. There wasn't much time to...play, like you do here."

He sat back a little in his seat. "I think you do your fair share of playing."

I eyed him uneasily. "What does that mean?"

He glanced over at my camera. Picked it up, his attitude casual.

My heart dropped down to my toes.

He paused to give me a little smile, then pressed a button and turned it on.

"Put that down," I demanded, my cheeks burning. A wave of heat flushed through my veins.

He glanced at me, his expression measuring. All at once, I became aware of a suppressed energy about him, a dangerous new glint to his eyes. He shifted in the chair and began to review the pictures. I watched, unable to speak, as he smiled, nodded, and offered small comments on each photo as he clicked through them: "Interesting," and, "Vanessa would be thrilled to see how good she looks here," and "Nice shot, that one," and "Mmmm." When he finally turned it off and put it back on the desk, he was frowning.

"So...you went to Beau Paradis, and saw me there with Vanessa."

I lifted my chin and nodded. An apology trembled on my lips, but I couldn't seem to say the words. "Is Vanessa your girlfriend?"

"Vanessa Scorizio is a friend," he said in clipped tones, then cocked an eyebrow. "Why didn't you leave when you saw us? Or make some noise to let us know you were there?"

I looked down at the sheet and pleated it between my suddenly-trembling fingers. He probably thought I was an unrepentant little beyotch, a damned liar spinning tales about my modesty and sensibility. "Uh..."

"Do you remember the story I told you about my tutor?" he asked softly, after a moment.

My eyes widening, I met his gaze and nodded.

"I took photos of her once, and when she saw them, she yanked my pants down, turned me over her knee, and spanked me until I begged for mercy."

My breath caught in my throat. I glanced at the door. To get there, I'd have to get past him. And the glint in his eye told me he wasn't going to allow any such thing.

And did I really want to get past him?

"Looks like you need the same lesson," he told me, his voice like steel.

I stared at him, unable to say a thing in my defense. I was guilty, and now he'd caught me red-handed, too. "What do you mean? I'm not a child.

You can't spank me."

"You've been acting like a child. A spanking is exactly what you deserve."

I tensed. I was seeing a new Jon here, a strict man, one more than happy to deliver punishment when it was appropriate. My gut instinct was to balk at his suggestion that I needed a spanking. And yet, another part of me—a more primal part—thrilled to his masterful tone, to the determination and arrogance in his face.

"Come over here." His eyes glittered darkly with something hot and seductive. I knew then that he wanted to spank me...maybe badly.

I pulled the sheet up higher. I could hardly breathe.

"The choice is yours," he said casually. "You can come over here and do as I've requested, or not. Whatever you decide, it won't affect your job. However...it will definitely affect our relationship."

"That's not fair," I accused.

He lifted an eyebrow, the expression in his face telling me he didn't care if it was fair or not.

For a second, I hesitated, and that second seemed to hang in the balance. It lasted far longer than it should. I'd been hoping for this kind of interest from him all last night. Right now, every cell in my body demanded I throw myself on his lap and lift my butt high in the air, so he could spank it, hard and long.

And yet...the doubts came, as they always did. Now that I was getting what I wanted--some extra-close attention from Jon--I thought of a new question to torture myself with. Did it really make sense for me to jeopardize my career at B3, by having sex with the boss? I tried to decide, but the truth was, I couldn't think at all. The only thing registering for me was the way his face had tightened with excitement, with desire as he waited.

I sucked in a deep breath. It was time to exercise that stiff upper lip Maine natives were renowned for, I told myself. To make the best of harsh conditions. I threw the sheet off.

He smiled, as if my decision had amused him in some way.

Slightly annoyed by his amusement, I slid off the bed and strolled over to him. If I was going to let him spank me, I refused to give him the upper hand in any other way. I'd take it like a woman, and get up with my chin lifted after it was done. "All right. Go ahead."

"Lift your nightgown up," he said, his face stern.

My fingers trembling, I gathered the fabric up between my fingers and slowly pulled my nightgown higher, then higher still. It took me a while. When I had it up as far as my thighs, I hesitated. My pussy was aching and my cheeks burned. I didn't know how long I'd be able to bare myself to him like that.

He raised an eyebrow.

I swallowed and slowly lifted my nightgown the rest of the way, until I had it bunched around my waist. I felt terribly vulnerable and exposed.

He stared at my face, at the blush that colored my cheeks, then dropped his gaze to my pussy. He examined me for a deliciously long time, until I was burning with excitement. Unable to take it any longer, I started to press my thighs together.

"Keep your legs spread," he demanded.

I swallowed, hard, and stood there, my pussy so wet that moisture slicked the insides of my thighs. My pulse was pounding, and my entire body hot with anticipation and embarrassment. With a defiant gaze, I dared him to make the next move.

He met my gaze head-on, his attitude relaxed; and then deliberately dropped his attention to the dark curls between my thighs. While I fidgeted uncomfortably, he studied my breasts, my legs, my pussy, and then my face once again. Finally, he sat up straighter. "Bend over my lap."

I glanced between his legs and saw a telltale bulge between them. My body growing even hotter, I slowly, reluctantly, laid down across his muscular lap. I felt his erection pushing into my stomach, with his legs as solid as tree trunks on either side. Cool air caressed my exposed skin. I trembled, my breasts hidden by the nightgown and hanging freely against his thigh.

He fondled my bottom with his palms, spreading my cheeks apart to look at my most secret places. I'd looked at myself in the mirror before from that angle, and knew what he was seeing: two plump pussy lips and a little pink bud between them. My sense of vulnerability grew, even as my pussy quivered with desperate yearning. Off balance, I clung to him for support and squirmed uncomfortably.

"Lay still," he ordered.

I wiggled a little more, suddenly angry that he was punishing me like this, and even angrier that I'd agreed to it. Still, I didn't move.

He traced his finger around my butt cheeks, and then dragged one between them, brazenly, until he touched my moist pussy and teased it with his fingertip. "You're very wet," he observed. "You must enjoy being spanked."

"Just get it over with," I demanded, completely humiliated.

I felt him lift his hand. Then, without warning, he brought it down sharply on my bottom, making a popping noise like a firecracker. I jerked at the blow and cried out at the hot, stinging pain. I hadn't realized it would hurt that badly. "Hey," I muttered. "Not so hard."

He chuckled and caressed my backside again, his touch unexpectedly gentle.

I fidgeted and tried to get up, but he held me down with a hand on my back and quickly administered another four spanks, each one as hard as the last. And every time his palm connected with my backside, it smarted like a smack from a paddle. I squirmed and choked back a sob and realized my pussy was aching worse than ever.

Then he paused. But he wasn't done with me yet.

"You won't take any more photos of me," he grated, the anger in his voice evident now.

Spank!

"Without my permission."

Spank!

I wiggled and squirmed on his lap.

"You won't lie to me," he continued.

Spank!

"And you won't withhold information."

Spank!

"Do I make myself clear?"

I gasped and nodded and made a little sobbing noise that sounded pathetic, even to my ears.

"Tell me that you understand."

"I understand," I mumbled.

"Good girl." He caressed my skin, which felt like

it was on fire. "I think you've learned your lesson. That's exactly what my tutor said to me all those years ago, by the way."

My bottom stung terribly, but the shame was worse. I looked back at him through a silvery blur of tears I couldn't control.

He reached forward to wipe the tears off my skin. Then his hand slid lower. He cupped my breast, gave it a little squeeze, then brushed my nipple. "That wasn't so bad, was it?"

"It was bad," I choked out, between a few fresh sobs.

Without warning, he leaned forward to plant a kiss on my red bottom. His lips felt cool, and firm, and all at once I wanted him to throw me on the bed and fuck my pussy as hard as he could. Wanting to hide, and wanting to be closer to him, I pressed my face against his lower abdomen. I felt his cock right beneath my chin. He felt rock hard, and the heat of it went right through his trousers.

"You need to be spanked more," he murmured. "It makes you very soft and sweet."

I wiggled off his lap. Then I flounced over to the bed and sat down, my sore bottom a reminder of what had just happened. "I really am sensible and modest," I insisted. "That's the way I was raised. Only down here...with you...everything's different. Everything's crazy! I don't even know myself anymore."

His lips quirked in a smile. "You're very different."

I lifted my chin.

"Nat said you were different," he added.

"How am I different?"

"You're way out of your element."

I swallowed, feeling scared, vulnerable....and more excited than I'd ever been before in my life. "Gee, that's encouraging."

He stood and picked up a particularly pretty bouquet of lush, overblown magenta flowers and roses; one that was tied with a pink velvet ribbon at the end. His gaze never leaving mine, he walked to my side, then sat on the edge of my bed. Carefully, gently, he laid the flowers on my lap. Their perfume washed over me, their colors wildly extravagant against the white sheets. I looked at the flowers, and then I looked at him. He held my gaze for a long, long time. His eyes mesmerized me--they were such a brilliant blue, and so intense. He seemed to see directly into my soul.

"You have a certain kind of naiveté," he finally said. "An honesty that I like."

I furrowed my brow as I took the rose from him. "Thanks?"

He smiled. "You have the potential to be one of our greatest creative assets. But right now, you have too many boundaries. You need to take a risk. Stop playing it so safe."

"You just spanked me," I pointed out. "That has to be taking a risk."

"It's a start," he agreed.

"Am I still your employee?"

His eyes crinkled at the corners with laughter. "Of course."

Suddenly, I remembered the photo shoot Nat had set up for this morning. I sat up straight, and looked at him with wide eyes. "I just remembered--I'm supposed to go to Beau Paradis this morning, to take photos. Nat convinced the site manager to hold off on construction until the afternoon. I'm already late!"

"Don't worry about it," he said. "I have some places I want to show you today. You'll do the shoot tomorrow."

"But my boss, Natalie—"

"I'll speak to Nat and our construction manager about it."

I wondered why he kept saying Nat in such a fond way. Had she been intimate with him? Did she still have a claim on him? Suddenly, I thought it must be so, and a deep unhappiness wound through me. "It sounds like you and Nat have quite a history," I observed.

He chuckled a little. "I'd say we do. Nat's my sister."

My mouth fell open. At the same time, I felt a sharp prick against my finger and realized I'd poked myself with one of the rose's thorns.

"Didn't she tell you?" he asked, genuinely surprised.

I shook my head no and glanced down at my thumb, which had a big drop of blood on top of it.

He saw the blood, too, and stood to get a washcloth from the bathroom. His expression neutral, he took my hand in his and examined my thumb, then stroked it lightly with the washcloth, his fingers caressing my skin, his touch stirring tantalizing sensations anew. At that moment, I sensed a new intimacy bloom between us, but I wanted more. I needed more.

I leaned toward him, looked up at him, begged him with my eyes to kiss me, to throw me back on the mattress and make me his.

He put the washcloth down, then grasped my arms

and moved me backward. "Get dressed, Demmie."

I sucked in a breath and stared at him, hurt.

He shifted away from the bed, sat back down, and started typing into his cell phone. "I'll give you ten minutes."

I climbed off the bed and stood in front of him, trembling. "I'll meet you in the lobby?"

"I'll wait here." He glanced my way, his gaze lingering on my nipples, which pressed against the thin cotton of my nightgown, then sighed with impatience.

I jumped to obey him, and wished I knew what I could do to provoke him into kissing me. How the hell did anyone go about seducing a man like Jon Baxter? It was a question I planned to devote myself to answering over the next few days.

But right now, I had to get dressed, before I annoyed him further. I took a second to gaze at his handsome face, to take in every inch of his six-foot-four frame, and silently, giddily congratulate myself on my phenomenal luck. Then I scrambled around my hotel room, looking for my clothes, my bottom still smarting from his spanking. He wanted to show me some things today, he'd said. I couldn't wait to see what he had in mind.

Quickly, I finished dressing—I had the white gauze dress on again—and slipped my sandals on. I put my hair up into a loose bun, patted some makeup on, and th[illegible] walked to his side. "I'm ready."

[illegible] d his cell phone call and stood. "Grab [illegible] ou're going to need it."

[illegible] we going?"

[illegible] wer. Instead, he started walking away, [illegible] his cell phone again. I picked up my camera bag and tripod, and then hurried out the door behind him, pausing only long enough to make sure I had my room key.

CHAPTER SEVEN

Jon and I walked out of the hotel and into the morning Miami sunshine. There, at the curb, sat two crazy-looking Jeep Wranglers, both two-seaters without a roof or doors, almost like dune buggies.

When Jon saw me looking at them, he grinned. He looked very playful. Very boyish.

I smiled, too. I couldn't help it. He was so damned hot...and completely charming. "Wow. Impressive!"

Both Jeeps had a bench seat in yellow and black up front, and a storage area where the back seats were normally located. Being somewhat familiar with off-road trucks—they were a requirement for getting around in snowy Maine winters—I had more than a passing appreciation for the car's suspension system. I could see it not only had all-wheel drive, but also looked capable of climbing side-by-side with a goat accustomed to prancing along the slopes of the Rocky Mountains.

"But why do we need two of them?" I asked.

Just then, I noticed a dark-haired woman walking through the lobby toward us. She was dressed in a lacy cover-up that revealed peeks of a pure white bikini, had two blonde guys with her--beach bum types.

Vanessa, I thought, unsettled.

"After you ran away last night," he replied casually, "I spoke to Vanessa. I took the liberty of mentioning you to her, and asked if she'd be interested in joining us today."

I bristled a little. Last night, he'd asked Vanessa to join 'us' even though I'd ditched him and taken a taxi back to my hotel. He'd been that confident of me. This, I reminded myself, was a man who always got his way. I adopted the coolest attitude I owned. "Should I have brought a bathing suit?"

"Do you have one?"

"No," I admitted, after a slight hesitation. Even if I had brought my board shorts and rash guard, I never would have worn them. I'd have looked like a frumpy old granny next to Vanessa.

"I didn't think so." He eyed my body boldly, his gaze lingering on my breasts and legs. "You won't need one, anyway."

I sent a startled glance his way. Vanessa was wearing a bathing suit. Why wouldn't I need one? Was I supposed to swim in my panties? Before I could even think of an appropriate question to ask him, however, he was nodding towards Vanessa's boy toys.

"Her two friends are Nat and Jordy. They're both from SoCal, and are on the USA's Olympic Volleyball Team. You'll see them playing at the next summer Olympics."

I nodded casually, though inside, I was very impressed. I looked at the beach bums with new eyes—took my time studying their leanly-muscled bodies, their deep tans, and their shaggy blonde hair. They were very cute, and also a perfect foil for

Vanessa, with her rippling black hair and haughty good looks.

I glanced back at Jon, and saw a glint of amusement in his eyes. I realized he'd been watching me check out the boy toys. My cheeks grew warm with embarrassment.

He pulled out a pair of sunglasses and put them on. "The Jeeps are my favorite ride when I'm down here in Miami."

He dug into his pocket, pulled out a second pair of sunglasses and handed them to me. I held them for a moment and looked at them: they had diamond chips on the nose bridge and across the top bar. Along the inside of the temples, which looked to be made of tortoiseshell or some kind of horn, the words Luxuriator Lux Due were stamped.

"Put them on," he said.

I slid them onto my face and gazed through lenses with a slightly pinkish sheen. I realized he'd given me rose-colored glasses. The world did, indeed look good through them. "They're nice."

Seconds later, Vanessa reached us, her two volleyball players flanking her on either side. Now that I had this close-up look at her, I could see that she was beautiful, indeed, with high cheekbones, a straight nose, and almond-shaped eyes that suggested she might have some Native American blood in her. She also had some serious money--I the clunky amethyst and diamond necklace around her neck looked to be worth tens of thousands.

She glanced briefly at me, her gaze cool, before she focused on Jon. "Which Jeep is mine?"

Jon grinned and held up two sets of keys. "Take your pick."

She took a set, and then the three of them hopped into the Jeep. Jordy took the wheel, and then they were off, the Jeep's back wheels spitting up gravel as they accelerated away.

Jon and I climbed into the remaining Jeep, I stowed my camera equipment, and we put our seatbelts on. Once he made sure I was securely fastened in, he stomped on the gas, and we were away like a shot. I gripped the handholds for dear life.

"Where's your goons and limo?" I asked, above the noise of the engine and the outdoors rushing past my ears. "Don't you need them around?"

"I'm giving them the day off," he shouted back.

"You just want to be normal today?"

He grinned.

We squealed through a couple of streets, but he couldn't remain at that initial high-spirited pace once we reached Ocean Drive. We kept the other Jeep in view as we drove down the thoroughfare, which became progressively more crowded the further south we went. Once we reached the end of South Beach, we took the bridge to the mainland.

Throughout that first part of the drive, Jon and I didn't talk much. The noise from the crowds on the sidewalk and from the other cars made a normal conversation nearly impossible. I settled for gawking at the art-deco hotels on either side of me, and the sports cars that prowled the road next to us. When I felt I could manage it without being noticed, I stole little glances at Jon, too. He looked so carefree, so at home behind the wheel, with the wind ruffling his hair and the sun burnishing it a dark dull gold, that I wanted to snuggle up next to him and just breathe him in.

I settled for asking him where we were headed, after we turned onto a highway.

"Key Biscayne," he answered, his grip on the steering wheel loose as we headed southeast.

"What's in Key Biscayne?"

"I need you to take a few photos for me there."

"Okay," I said, intrigued at the thought of him needing photos.

Jon stepped on the gas, and seconds later we were rocketing past Vanessa's Jeep. Jordy waved to us as we passed by, and then they fell in behind us. I settled back against the seat and let the Miami warmth and sunshine warm my skin. I took in the palm trees and the greenery, which got progressively wilder as we approached yet another bridge that spanned the turquoise depths of Biscayne Bay.

I breathed in salt air as we crossed the bay, drove briefly on a small island, and then crossed another bridge over a wider stretch of water. After several minutes, we reached an island with signs naming it Key Biscayne. The highway became an avenue that led us past million-dollar mansions and five-star hotels.

"We're heading to the southernmost point of the island," he told me, as we cruised down the avenue. "I have a small place down there, in the state park—it's accessible only by driving along the beach. I think you'll like it. But first, we're going to stop at The Nail."

"What's 'The Nail?'"

"A beach shack," he replied. "It's one of Vanessa's favorite bars down here."

We continued along the road, until the houses and hotels gave way to sand dunes and scrubby beach brush. The road itself turned to gravel, and seagulls swooped back and forth above us as they flew around looking for lunch. I realized we'd entered the state park, and it wasn't long afterward that I heard smooth, easy Jimmy Buffet-style rock and roll coming out of a dilapidated-looking building with weathered gray shingles. It sat right on the edge of the Atlantic Ocean and had an attached terrace, on which people were dancing.

Jon pulled into the building's parking lot. I saw a sign that said The Rusty Nail and knew we'd arrived at Vanessa's favorite dive. Her Jeep pulled in behind us, and then we all went inside. Heads turned as soon as Vanessa walked in; her lace beach cover-up didn't cover much. Jordy and Nat circled protectively around her, and Jon ordered a round of drinks from the waitress.

I looked around, entranced. This wasn't a place for the rich and famous to hang out. No, just regular people rubbed shoulders here--girls dressed in super-short cutoffs and tank tops, and guys in jeans, with landscaping logos on their T-shirts. The beer flowed freely and everyone seemed to have at least one tropical-looking mixed drink in hand. In the corner, a band was playing country-rock music, and a few people were dancing on the terrace.

The waitress brought me a daiquiri—Jon had obviously remembered me drinking one at the hotel and had ordered the same for me here. Vanessa had a tumbler filled with an amber liquid, and both Jordy and Nat had beers. Jon's glass appeared to hold club soda. I drank my daiquiri pretty quickly, my foot tapping in time with the music, and he promptly ordered me another.

He stood very close to me as we drank, and chatted about the 'small home' he owned at the tip of the island. I smiled and let his appeal wash over me like a warm ocean wave. More than once since I'd met him, he'd seemed an arrogant, remote man; but at the moment, he was completely relatable, somewhat quiet but undeniably sexy, and even a little bit vulnerable. I laughed at something he said and bumped up against him and smiled into his deep blue eyes. My heart beat out a quick rhythm in my chest when he smiled back, and I silently admitted I was completely and utterly infatuated.

And so, when a dark-haired, muscled guy in jeans and a T-shirt with its sleeves cut off nudged toward me and tried to start a conversation, I felt more than a little surprised. Hadn't he seen Jon and me with our heads together, talking?

"Wanna dance?" the muscled guy asked, his breath smelling like a distillery.

I glanced with something close to alarm at Jon, but he simply smiled and gave me a little push toward the dance floor. "Go ahead."

The muscled guy leaned close, his arm brushing against the side of my breast as we left the bar and walked outside, onto the terrace. The sunshine reflected an invitation in his gaze, one I couldn't fail to see. "I'm Greg," he said. "I saw you standing over there with your brother. You looked like you needed to dance."

"He's not my brother," I informed him.

He wrapped an arm around my waist and pulled me closer. "Is he your boyfriend, then? You looked nervous, little lady."

"No, he's not my boyfriend," I said coolly. "And I

wasn't nervous."

He picked up my hand and put it on his shoulder. "What is he, then? Your dad?" He guffawed at his own joke, while I just rolled my eyes with annoyance.

We started hopping around the dance floor....me, reluctantly, and my partner with too much eagerness. I realized then that the guy—Greg—was more than a little drunk. I looked toward the bar, hoping to see Jon, and caught a glimpse of him near the door, watching. I sent him an alarmed look, one laced with humor, because Greg was gyrating like Elvis on crack and making a complete spectacle of himself.

Jon smiled faintly, but otherwise remained standing near the door, watching me, studying me, assessing.

Obviously he wasn't going to rescue me. He just wanted to watch.

All at once, I felt like I had something to prove. I suddenly needed to show Jon that I wasn't a complete stick in the mud...that I knew how to dance and flirt just like the rest of the female species. I gave Greg a big smile, summoned some enthusiasm and relaxed a little. I made a point of working my hips a tad more, rolling my body a little.

"Woah, baby," Greg said, after I'd put some effort into it.

My smile faltered when he pressed up against me a little harder.

"Are you here by yourself?" I asked him loudly, and tried to put an extra inch or two between us.

"No, I'm here with my buddies. My best friend's getting married. We decided to stop here before heading up to Miami."

I tensed. A bachelor party. Nothing good came

of a bunch of guys with liquor and sex on their minds. Abruptly I realized that Greg was not the guy I wanted to prove myself with. I pulled away an inch or so more and glanced over at Vanessa.

She was also on the dance floor, between Jordy and another guy I didn't recognize, someone who looked like he typically spent at least half a day lifting weights. Both my and Vanessa's new partner were sexy in an aggressive, low-class way, and they both seemed to enjoy staring at our breasts—although Vanessa's partner could have been eyeing up that clunky necklace at her throat.

I caught her gaze, and she widened her eyes in a put-upon way, then gave me a little wink.

I smiled back. She was enjoying herself, I thought. And suddenly, I kind of liked her.

Still, I couldn't relax. Greg kept trying to pull me closer, and didn't seem to respect the fact that I just wanted to dance, and nothing more. I felt his hands run up and down my back, before settling against my skin, and I stiffened. "I need a rest," I told him, and tried to escape.

But he held me fast. "What?" he shouted. "The music's still playing! You can't go now." And he gyrated more wildly against me.

"No, I'm done," I said sharply.

He didn't seem to hear me, and pulled me in closer, until my nipples brushed against his chest.

I felt my nipples harden from the contact and blushed. "Let me go." I yanked at his arms, but couldn't get him to loosen his grip.

"Oh, come on. I know chicks like you," he replied.

"Where's your girlfriend?" I asked, changing tactics. "Would she appreciate it if she saw you on me like this?"

"This ain't about my girlfriend." His whiskey-sour breath washed over me. "I know your type. You act like a kindergarten teacher, but really, you're thinking about how much you want it." He shifted back just enough to get a good look at my hardened nipples, then added, "Relax, baby."

"Look, you're drunk, and you're making a mistake. Just let me go."

He laughed aloud. "No way." And then his arms were tight around me, the rough cotton of his T-shirt rubbing against my bare arms as he crushed me against him, flattening my breasts against his chest. He lowered his face to my neck and nuzzled there, his breath a hot attack against my skin.

"Hey, stop it," I choked out, and then wondered how much more space I'd need to jam my knee up into his balls.

Without warning, a heavy hand landed against my partner's shoulder.

I gasped aloud and stared into the blue eyes across from me.

Jon!

Greg grunted with confusion and lifted his head from my neck. For just one second, he had a shocked, deer-in-the-headlights look.

"The lady said she's done." Jon was in complete control of himself. Although his face was taut, and he'd set his mouth in a tight line, he appeared calm. Remote. Superior to everyone else in the room. And somehow, that calm superiority made him all the more threatening. More dangerous. Unpredictable. And goddamned sexy.

Greg's face twisted with an almost comical look of

belligerence. He pulled me in closer. "She ain't done. We're just getting started."

I craned my neck to get away from his stale breath.

Jon settled a cold look on Greg. "Let her go."

"The music ain't over yet, bro."

"For you, it is," Jon replied casually. "And I'm not your bro."

My partner abruptly released me and swung wildly at Jon. I stumbled to the side as Jon blocked the punch effortlessly, as though he got into fistfights every day. Then, with lightning-fast moves, he shot a quick left fist toward Greg's chin, knocking his head to the side, then followed up with a right cross hand punch to the same. Greg lurched backward, his face slack, and Jon finished him off with a side kick to his gut. Greg went sprawling across the dance floor, knocking into several people before landing on his butt.

Hisses and gasps of surprise filled the dance floor. People started backing away and looking for the source of the fight. I cast a panicked glance toward the bar. One of the bar tenders had pulled a baseball bat out from under the bar.

Another guy who'd been dancing nearby suddenly came up behind Jon and laid a punch on the back of his head. Jon must have sensed it coming, and ducked his head at the last second, and the guy staggered forward. Jon raised a knee just at the right moment, and the guy careened into Jon's knee. At the same time, across the dance floor, the guy who'd been dancing with Vanessa made a grab at her necklace, and she yelped with surprise.

Jordy threw a quick punch at the would-be thief and hustled Vanessa off the dance floor. Jon grabbed my arm, and Nat brought up the rear. Before I really knew quite what had happened, we were racing out of The Rusty Nail, with several guys from the bachelor party running after us and cursing at us the whole time. Behind them, the bartender followed with his baseball bat in hand, and a beefy-looking bouncer trailed him.

All of a sudden, I was wishing for Jon's goons and limo.

"Come on, let's get the sonofabitch!" Greg yelled.

Running for my life, and with Jon urging me on faster, we made it to the Jeep and jumped in. Jon turned the key and the Jeep roared to life. Nat, Jordy and Vanessa got to theirs a second later, and then we were both pulling out of the parking lot, and spitting gravel everywhere.

I saw the bachelor party crew run to their own cars. They were going to give chase.

"Holy shit," I breathed, my adrenaline pumping. "They're going to follow us."

"Good luck," Jon bit out, as our Jeep nearly skidded out, then caught the gravel road and leapt forward.

I thought he would turn toward the main road, but instead, he sent the car in the opposite direction, away from the town. The road looked like little more than a path in this direction, and dense foliage and palm trees on either side turned it into a green tunnel. Jordy kept right on our bumper in the other Jeep. And a little way back, I saw the bachelor party boys pull out in a pickup truck.

"Where are we going?" I yelled, as Jon accelerated and the Jeep flew over a bump in the road.

"Somewhere they can't go," he yelled back, and

abruptly, the gravel road gave way to sand, and the greenery flanking us on either side fell away, revealing a sparkling sand beach, foaming waves, and the Atlantic Ocean further out.

Upon our appearance, a few seagulls took flight, but otherwise the beach appeared deserted.

The Jeep hit the beach, and then John made a sharp right, sending sand upward in a spray. The car's tires caught immediately and we shot forward, with Jordy hot on our trail. I turned around and saw the pickup truck barrel onto the beach also, but before it had gone more than twenty feet, its rear wheels got stuck in the sand.

Jon slowed down and studied the pickup in his rear-view mirror. The pickup's driver was hitting the accelerator, and in doing so, digging the pickup's wheels further in.

They weren't going anywhere.

I sagged back against the seat and passed a trembling hand over my forehead. "Maybe you shouldn't have given your goons the day off."

"I'm sure they'll be pissed to hear that they missed out on the action."

I frowned. "Do you get in trouble like this a lot?"

He turned toward me, his eyes gleaming, and tucked a stray tendril of my hair behind my ear. "Not usually. You must be the one bringing it."

"Right." I was still shaking in the aftermath of all the violence, and my first instinct was to yell at him. Was he crazy, starting a fight like that? But then, I remembered the look on Greg's face when Jon had put his hand on Greg's shoulder—that shocked, deer-in-the-headlights look—and I chuckled. Jon smiled too, and after a moment, we were both laughing.

When we finally got it under control, Jon slowed the Jeep even further, until we were creeping along at the edge of the surf. Jordy pulled up next to us, and Jon looked the three of them over. "Everyone okay?"

"You're nothing but fun, Jon," Vanessa said, her voice amused.

He smiled and ducked his head, and I fought an instant feeling of jealousy.

"I hadn't planned on getting onto the beach this quickly," he told me, "but we're heading in the right direction. My cottage is just another mile or so down."

□

CHAPTER EIGHT

We arrived at Jon's 'cottage' a few minutes later. Of course, it hadn't anything in common with any kind of cottage I knew. The place was two stories high and constructed mostly of windows, with stucco between them and a ridged metal roof covering it all. It sat several hundred feet back from the beach, amidst a grove of palm and coconut trees, and had a large deck, complete with patio umbrellas, teak furniture, a gazebo filled with floor pillows, an outdoor fireplace and a bar. As we parked the Jeeps on the beach and hopped out, I counted two pools: both rectangular, lined and edged with small turquoise glass tiles that sparkled in the sunlight.

"Some cottage," I murmured, as Jon walked up a path that crossed over a dune.

He glanced around and waved me on with one hand. "Come on in."

My camera bag in hand, I followed him up the path, with Nat, Jordy and Vanessa behind me. When we reached the deck, a gray-haired, distinguished looking man in a white suit met us.

"Welcome home, Mr. Baxter," the man said.

Jon smiled and nodded. "Thank you, Linton." He glanced at me. "Linton takes care of the place when I'm gone."

I nodded toward Linton, who also inclined his head in my direction.

Vanessa pushed forward until she stood next to Jon. "Can we get a few drinks?"

Jon transferred his attention to Linton. "Grab us a few bottles of champagne, Linton?"

"Of course, sir," Linton replied pleasantly. "Will you be needing me this afternoon?"

"No, you can go."

Linton inclined his head again, this time toward Jon, and then he disappeared into the house, presumably to get the champagne.

Vanessa lifted one black, arched eyebrow. "Would you like me to show Demmie around, Jon?"

He shrugged. "I'll take Nat and Jordy over to the gazebo."

Vanessa turned toward me and curled her lips in a feline-looking smile. "He has quite a place here. You're going to like it."

I forced my lips into an answering smile, although my stomach felt sour. If she knew this place well enough to 'show me around,' then she'd clearly been here several times.

She hooked her arm through mine and, her long black hair brushing up against me, steered me into the house. Our tour began in a vaulted foyer with a big Aubusson rug on the floor and a metal-and-glass staircase leading upstairs. She pointed out a few objects d'art and then strolled into a gourmet kitchen, where she further demonstrated her knowledge of his home. After a few minutes, I realized that she wanted me to understand that she and Jon had been more than just friends for a long time.

As we walked into a living room, she paused in

front of a gigantic silver-framed wall mirror. Naturally, I paused with her, and we assessed our images: Vanessa, tall and willowy, with those high Native American cheekbones and gleaming black hair; and me, short, with a mass of wavy brown hair that refused to stay put, and big boobs that made me look, in my opinion at least, top-heavy.

Ugh.

When she moved us past the mirror, I breathed a sigh of relief...and also felt properly put in my place.

She patted my arm as we started up the stairs to the second floor. "So...Jon tells me you're a very gifted photographer."

I nodded cautiously. "I won B3's photography contest. That's how I got this job in the first place."

"Very nice." She led me down the second floor hallway to a bedroom. We peeked inside, then moved on. "But how many nude photo shoots have you done?" she asked.

I stumbled a little. "Nude photo shoots?"

She smiled and brought me to a second bedroom with a coffered wood ceiling, windows on three of the walls and two queen-sized beds. "Yes. Nude."

"Why do you ask?"

She gazed at me with wide eyes. "Didn't Jon tell you?"

A tendril of anxiety stirred in my gut. "Tell me what?"

"Jon promised me that you'd do my shoot with Nat and Jordy. But if you would prefer not to—"

I sensed she was looking for a way to get rid of me and cut right in, despite my uneasiness. "No, that's fine."

We passed into a small study, with a desk, a futon,

a map of the world on the wall, and a straw fedora hanging off the edge of a wooden shelf. "Will you both, er, all three of you be nude?" I asked.

"We'll be dressed at first. But then...you'll see." She chuckled in a self-deprecating way. "It's a whim of mine—I love getting dressed up and posing for photographs, but it can be hard to find a competent photographer, one who has the talent to catch the interesting shot, the different shot."

Suddenly I felt all kinds of pressure. This was not going to be an easy woman to please. And I knew she'd be vocal if she wasn't satisfied. I put my hand on a dresser for support. "So, this is a striptease act of some sort?"

She laughed. "Nothing so vulgar."

"Okay," I replied, but inside, I was saying a little prayer of thanks.

She tilted her head thoughtfully. "I want sexy, Demmie. I want hot. Can you do that for me?"

I nodded.

"I don't like it when people falsely represent themselves," she continued.

I pulled my arm from hers. "You're just going to have to wait and see."

She examined me closely, as if she didn't believe me, then shrugged and led me into what had to be the master bedroom. This bedroom had a coffered wood ceiling with a fan in the middle, but instead of windows on all sides, it had only two large built-in windows. Both had window seats with cushions that looked to be the size of a single bed. A large king-sized bed dominated the room, and shelves covered any part of the walls that didn't have windows. I saw multitudes of knick-knacks on the shelves—a beer stein from Germany, an Australian flag, a bottle of Russian vodka—all manners of items that appeared to be from different parts of the world.

"This is Jon's bedroom, when he's here," Vanessa informed me needlessly.

I wandered over to a shelf that contained silver-framed photos. I saw an older couple, possibly Jon's parents; as well as one of Jon flanked on either side by two men—the Baxter brothers, I guessed. But the one that interested me the most was of a younger woman, about my age maybe, with brown curly hair similar to mine. I picked the photo up and studied it.

"Who is this?" I asked Vanessa.

She walked over to my side and looked at it. "That's Sarah. His first wife."

My insides thrumming with surprise, I put the photo down. "I hadn't realized he'd been married."

"He was until a few years ago. We'd better get downstairs before Jon wonders what happened to us." Vanessa spun around and walked away, and I realized that I'd heard all I was going to on the subject, at least from her.

I followed her downstairs, and we quickly made our way out to the gazebo. Vanessa immediately strolled to Jon's side. Jordy and Nat were nowhere to be seen.

Vanessa shook her finger at Jon playfully. "You didn't tell Demmie what we want her to take photos of."

He glanced at me. "Any problems with shooting Vanessa nude?"

My cheeks heating, I shook my head no. Vanessa didn't know that I'd already photographed her nude; and now that I'd gotten to know her better, I seriously hoped Jon never told her.

Jon walked to a side table, where four bottles of champagne sat cooling in silver ice buckets, and grabbed a champagne bottle. He popped it open, poured each of us a glass of the frothy liquid, and handed them out. I took mine and sipped delicately, even though I wanted to gulp it down. I couldn't risk getting drunk, and then taking horrible photos.

"Why don't you get set up, Demmie," Jon suggested. "I'm sure Vanessa will want to touch up her makeup, too."

"If you don't mind, I'd like to take a final look at Vanessa's makeup right before we start," I replied. "Just to make sure it'll work well with the camera."

Vanessa shrugged. "Fine by me."

With that, I set up my tripod and messed around with my camera's controls until they reflected the settings I thought I'd need. I took several initial photographs of the gazebo itself, without anyone in it, and played some more with the settings until I'd made the most of the available light. I asked Jon to hang a sheet from one side of the gazebo, to diffuse the sunlight blazing through the trees, and then attached my camera to the tripod.

Vanessa appeared just as I was taking a few final test shots. I caught my breath when I saw her. She looked beautiful, with brilliant green eyes and those haughty cheekbones, and I understood all too well why Jon had decided to make love to her in Beau Paradis. She was a bird of paradise herself, in a gauzy green dress with a deep V-neck that revealed the swell of her breasts. I worked hard to stifle my feelings of jealousy as I went back to the makeup table with her. With a critical eye, I suggested a few changes to the way she'd shadowed her eyes and contoured her cheeks. After she'd made the changes, we returned to the gazebo.

Nat and Jordy were standing between the cushions, dressed in black tuxedos with their blonde hair slicked neatly back. I caught my breath at the sight of them, too. They were blonde, toned, handsome men who had an indefinable air of old money about them, of class and good breeding. They smiled at me, their teeth flashing white in their tanned faces.

"How do you want us?" Jordy asked.

All three of them were looking at me and waiting for my direction.

A little panicked, I glanced at Jon. He simply raised his eyebrows.

I swallowed. "Okay, how about you and Nat stand on either side of Vanessa, and put your arms around her?"

Jon moved off to the side. Jordy and Nat promptly followed my directions, and then gazed at me, ready for more. I focused on them through the camera viewfinder. I didn't think I'd ever had more beautiful people as subjects before. I told them to relax, to smile, to give me attitude, to move around naturally, and then took some photos.

They were gorgeous.

I glanced at Jon-- he was watching everything very closely. I recalled him telling me that I needed to start taking risks, to step outside of what I felt comfortable with, and knew that this was my chance to stand out. To show him what I was made of. To take photos that blew his socks off. The problem was, I had no idea how to guarantee 'sexy.' I downed another gulp of champagne.

"Do you have any other directions for us?" Jordy asked. He was standing there in his tuxedo, looking a little uncomfortable and waiting for me to act like a professional.

"Uhhh...move a little closer together."

They shuffled toward each other, and I wandered back and forth in front of them to snap some photos.

"Now what?" Nat asked.

I stared at him. Now what, indeed? Panic skittered through me. I opened my mouth to make some sort of apology, when suddenly, I saw Jon lean toward me. "I have a few ideas," he said, his breath warm against my ear. "Would you mind if I try them?"

"Please, go ahead," I said with a rush, and slumped a little with relief.

He walked toward the trio, his gaze on Vanessa. "Look at her," he said, to Nat and Jordy. "Look at how gorgeous she is. Her smile, her perfect skin..." He circled around her, assessing, studying. "Such long legs. Beautiful thighs. And spirited. Passionate."

Vanessa, I noticed, had a vulnerable look on her face, which surprised me...I thought she'd bask in Jon's attention. But rather, she seemed very feminine, and fragile. Both Nat and Jordy were staring at Vanessa now, their gazes intense, as if they were seeing her for the first time.

I felt a surge of admiration for my boss—he was coaxing emotion out of them, and emotion made any photo interesting, regardless of the subject.

Jon was careful to stay out of the photo's frame, and I discreetly took a few pictures. I didn't want to break the spell he was casting. But I almost dropped my camera when he moved to Vanessa's side and slipped the silk strap from her shoulder. Her dress immediately fell open and exposed one of her breasts, the milky white globe with its pink nipple a lush sight against her green gauze dress.

I quickly snapped a photo, as her mouth formed an 'O' of surprise. She grabbed the strap and started to pull it back up, but Jon stopped her.

"No," he said softly. "I want to look at you."

Slowly, her hand trembling slightly, she dropped the strap and stood there beneath his gaze. Jordy and Nat were staring, too. I watched her nipple harden. My own nipples felt achy and tingly.

"That's what you want, isn't it, Vanessa?" Jon asked. "You want us to look at you?"

She trembled a little and focused on the floor.

"Look at her, Jordy, Nat," Jon coaxed. "Do you see how hard her nipple is? She likes when people stare at her."

Vanessa glanced up and parted her lips to say something, but Jon immediately put a finger against his own lips. "Shhh. Don't speak," he ordered.

She closed her mouth and gave him a mute, puppy-like glance of adoration.

I realized I was trembling, too. I continued to take photos—quietly.

"Tell me: How does it work with the two of you?" he asked Nat and Jordy. "Do you feel jealous, Jordy, when Nat kisses her and you have to watch?"

A muscle flexed in Jordy's jaw.

"And how about you, Nat? How do you feel when Jordy puts his hand on Vanessa's breast, like this?" Jon grabbed Jordy's hand and guided it to Vanessa's exposed breast. He released Jordy's hand, but Jordy kept his hand on Vanessa's breast...he began to stroke the undersides of it, and then run his fingers across her nipple.

Nat frowned, his gaze locked on Jon's. Then, just slightly, he cut a glance toward Vanessa.

"That's right, Nat. Look at Vanessa. She likes it so much, the way Jordy's caressing her."

Nat's frown deepened.

"Does that annoy you, Nat? That she's enjoying the touch of another man?"

Vanessa's lower lip trembled. She leaned a little into Jordy's palm, the same way a cat moves closer to a petting hand.

Jon's gaze flickered between the three of them, his eyes dark, unreadable.

A few moments passed, during which Nat watched Jordy stroke Vanessa's breast, and I caught the whole scene digitally.

Jon's attention fastened on Vanessa. "And you, Vanessa. What happened to make you need two men in your bed?"

She stared back at him, her lower lip trembling harder, her eyes wide. But she didn't speak.

"Are you angry? Did your Greek billionaire husband make you angry?"

"Fuck you, Jon," she finally hissed. Two spots of color brightened her cheekbones.

I stilled. It hadn't even occurred to me that Vanessa might be married.

He smiled. "Be quiet."

Once again, she closed her mouth and focused on the floor.

He glanced out the window, as if searching for the right words, and then asked, "Did you find him with another woman?"

A tear suddenly rolled down Vanessa's cheek.

"Are you punishing him because he wanted someone else? Is that it?"

Another tear ran down her cheek, even as Jordy slid his palm around the curve of her breast and caressed her nipple. All at once, I felt bad for her, and uncomfortable about these secrets revealed.

"Has your husband pushed you into Jordy's and Nat's bed?"

She choked back an outright sob. I stopped taking photos and looked away.

Jon swiveled toward me and demanded harshly, "Do your job, Demmie."

My hands shaking, I grasped the camera and focused once more through the view finder.

He gave me a nod of satisfaction, then leaned closer to Vanessa and caught her gaze with his own. "When you found him, did he have his hands between her legs, like this?" He grabbed Nat's hand and guided it to rest between Vanessa's thighs. "Is that what happened?"

Nat began fondling her pussy through her dress. She sucked in a deep, excited breath and threw her head back, the tracks of her tears still wet on her cheeks. In that moment, she looked achingly gorgeous, her lashes spiked with tears, a pink flush on her cheeks and her breasts heaving with excitement. I focused in on her, snapped several pictures, and knew with a bittersweet kind of contentment that she'd have no regrets when she saw these photos.

Jordy leaned down and pressed a hard, passionate kiss against her neck. She arched against him, thrusting her breast further into his hand, even as Nat fondled her pussy with quick, needy motions. The three of them slowly collapsed to the pillows behind them, and then the two men were kissing her, one after the other, sharing her lips, teasing her with their tongues, and splitting the task of getting her dress off of her.

I photographed them, my heart thudding in my chest, feeling dizzy, feeling breathless as Nat stood and shucked his jacket, trousers, and boxers; revealing the bronzed, muscled body of an athlete. I felt Jon's gaze on me as I stared, open-mouthed, at Nat's thrusting erection, then took several photos of it in quick succession. When I glanced at Jon next, I saw that he was smiling—clearly he felt satisfied with the day's events and the reactions he'd orchestrated from each of us. But at the moment, I didn't care that I'd allowed him to manipulate me, because Jordy was taking his tuxedo off, and my God that man had a body that even a nun would salivate over.

Chewing my lower lip, and feeling of a sheen of sweat on my skin, I photographed the three of them—all nude, now—laying on the pillows, groping, touching, fondling. Some part of me felt ashamed, to be watching them like a voyeur...but another part couldn't get enough. I wondered if my dad were somehow watching me from Heaven and shaking his head with disgust.

They moaned and writhed around the pillows, all of their inhibitions gone in their pursuit of pleasure. I'd never felt completely uninhibited like that, and just as I wondered what it felt like, Nat moved between her legs. He spread her pussy lips and licked at her little pink bud with a firm tongue, while Jordy kneeled in front of her and slid his red, throbbing cock slowly into her mouth. I gasped and looked away, but then slowly glanced back as the shock wore off, and stared as she hungrily sucked Jordy's cock, even as she thrust her pussy towards Nat's mouth in an eager bid for more. After a minute of this, Jordy reached down to squeeze and caress her breasts, and she moaned deep in her throat.

That moan seemed to be a signal for the two men. Jordy pulled his cock from her mouth, and Nat flipped her over, onto her stomach. She lifted herself until she was kneeling on her hands and knees, and then Jordy slid his cock into her pussy, slowly, inch by inch, until she groaned and thrust her hips backwards, against his. Barely breathing, I took more photos, and then searched the room for Jon. I found him standing on the other side of the gazebo, across from me. His attention wasn't on the threesome writhing on the bed, but on me. I swallowed.

Jordy began riding her, his cock rigid like steel as he squeezed her full butt cheeks with his hands. Nat grasped his cock and kneel-walked forward until he was close to Vanessa's lips. She had her eyes closed, and didn't see him, so he held his cock out and rubbed its head against her lips. Her eyes snapped open, and her lips parted a moment later. He pushed his hard member into her mouth and threw his head back, his face contorted with pleasure, as she sucked him.

I stared at the tableau...aghast, shocked, turned on, forever changed. My camera forgotten, I glanced up at Jon, and our gazes locked over the sexual antics on the bed. His hands thrust into his pockets, he casually walked around the pillows, over to me.

"What do you think, Demmie?" he said softly, his

gaze never leaving mine.

"I...I don't know." I drew in a deep, shaky breath and tried not to hear the moans of pleasure on the bed.

"Have you ever felt like that before?" He lifted a hand and brushed his fingers along the curve of my jaw. "Lost in passion...primal...and desperate for release?"

I focused on the ocean, on the waves crashing up against the shore. I didn't know how to answer him, and I didn't want to watch any longer.

"Look at them," he said.

"No."

"Look at them."

I turned and dared to lock gazes with him. "I can't." But even as I said this, I swiveled to glance at the threesome on the pillows. They'd switched positions—Vanessa now sat on top of Jordy and was riding him, as Nat kissed her deeply, ferociously.

"What do you see?"

I swallowed and fought a sense of shame. "I see three people in a ménage a trois."

We stared at each other. I wanted to drop my gaze from his, but somehow I held steady. After a moment, Jon lifted an eyebrow. "That's right. They're having sex. Do you understand how it's different from making love?"

Vanessa pulled her lips from Nat's and began to moan, long and loud. Her face tightened with tension and she rode Jordy harder, faster, until finally, she shuddered and collapsed against him.

"There is no difference," I whispered, as Jordy flipped Vanessa over, moved between her thighs and plunged into her.

"Oh yes, there is." He nodded toward Vanessa. "They desire each other's bodies, but nothing else. They're having sex. When you make love, you desire the other person's body and soul. You join with the other person's body and soul, and become one. It's an entirely different experience."

I nodded slowly, my body thrumming with need for him, the champagne flowing through my veins like fire.

"Having sex is easy," he continued. "Making love is much more difficult."

I drew in a breath, gathered my courage, and asked, "Did you make love to your first wife?"

He tensed, glanced sharply at me, and then nodded. "I did."

"But somehow, it wasn't enough," I pressed. "Otherwise, you'd still be married."

"I suppose that's true." His heavy-lidded blue eyes took in my dress, my naked shoulders, my curly hair, which hung down in a riotous mass past my shoulders. I saw desire in them, one that he tried to conceal but couldn't. "The flames of love-making are quick to die if one person wants only sex. It's fake when it's based on pretense...when there's manipulation rather than authenticity."

"What would it be, between you and me?" I dared to ask, my entire body aquiver for him.

"I don't know," he replied, his voice a deep, husky rasp. "But I don't make love any more. I only have sex."

I frowned. "Why?"

"Because making love is too dangerous."

I'm not the marrying kind... I remembered him saying that. And now, he was saying that he only fucked, he never made love. That he would never share his heart with anyone, no matter how hard anyone tried to capture it. My frown deepened. I felt genuinely angry. "Why are you telling me all of this? Why all of this trouble?"

"You need to know. To understand."

"But why do I need to understand?" I gestured angrily at Vanessa, Nat and Jordy, who were kissing and cuddling on the pillows. "Why this lesson in 'having sex?' Why did we take this trip? Why are you in my life at all?"

"You interest me, Demmie," he murmured. "You're different, like a breath of fresh air. And yes, I want you. I can see you want me." He hesitated, looked away, then refocused on me. All of a sudden, I saw a coolness in his gaze. A remoteness. "But you need to realize," he continued, "that you and I will only have sex--you'll never have anything more. And I sense that you're the kind of woman who will always need more."

Finally. There it was. The invitation, the warning. He'd have sex with me if I wanted it. But he'd never fall in love with me. He would keep an invisible wall between us, always--

And yet, I hardly needed even a moment to decide what I wanted. I already knew. I'd known since the moment I'd watched him in Beau Paradis with Vanessa. I lifted my chin. "I want you to fuck me."

His eyes widened. "Do I have you all wrong, Demmie?"

"Maybe you do," I lied.

"Are you using birth control?"

"You need to ask me that?" I looked down my nose at him.

"Really." He lifted one eyebrow. "How do you like it, then? Rough? Do you want another spanking?"

I shrugged and piled more lies on. "I've had it lots of ways. Why don't you choose?"

A harsh glint sparked in his blue eyes. Without warning, he reached out, wrapped his arms around me and dragged me against him. I yelped, and opened my mouth to demand he put me down, but then his lips closed on mine in a deep, hungry kiss. His arm like a band of steel around my back, I felt jolt after jolt of burning excitement shoot through me as he brutally demanded my surrender.

Confused by his flagrant attack, I put my palm against his chest, but I didn't push away, because I didn't want the kiss to end. His tongue tangled with mine and he crushed my heaving chest against his; and after a long, long time, he lifted his head to look at me.

I swayed against him, dizzy.

He laughed, deep in his throat, and lifted my bodily from the ground. He swung me over his shoulder, violently, knocking what little breath I had from my lungs. I landed with a thud, shocked beyond words, my face pressed against his muscled back, his shoulder digging into my abdomen.

"This is how I want it," he informed me.

Determined to get down, I let out a croak and squirmed against him. Yes, I wanted him, but I didn't appreciate being manhandled like this.

He laughed again and smacked me sharply on the butt, then strode into the house.

"Just where do you think you're taking me?" I asked coolly, my butt in the air as he jostled me through the living room.

He gave a muttered laugh and marched up the stairs. "Where you want to go, sexy."

I drew in a little breath. I didn't like how he'd said the word sexy. Somehow, it had sounded like an insult. "Put me down, Jon."

He carried me into the master bedroom with the king-sized bed and set me down. Weak-kneed, I swayed on my feet. He made no effort to steady me. Instead, breathing heavily, he gestured toward the door. His eyes still held that steely, savage glint. "If you don't want to be here, feel free to leave."

Abruptly filled with conflicting emotions, I glanced at the door, then looked back at him. The anger inside me had begun to fade, changing into a languid, delicious ache, as though my blood had thickened and now coursed through my veins like warmed honey. And yet, I was also very aware that I was about to lose my virginity to man who'd said he'd never love me. Could I actually go through with this?

A mocking smile curled his lips. "I thought you'd stay."

I returned his stare, the ache he'd aroused in me far harder to ignore than my conscience.

He moved suddenly, pulling me to him. Instinctively I raised my hands. With a muttered grunt, he ignored the gesture and again crushed my lips with his, his kiss fierce and demanding. My hands were useless, pinned between our bodies, and all at once, I felt trapped. I squirmed against him, my thighs straining against his, and the hard lump of his erection pressed against me, even as his tongue jabbed into my mouth and tangled with mine. Over and over again he kissed me, his lips wearing down my instinctive resistance, making me forget that I was a virgin, and demanding that I give in.

All at once, I could take no more. I melted against him with a wantonness I hadn't realized I was capable of. We fell to the mattress, his body on top of mine. My lips opened lushly beneath his and I twined my arms around him as I writhed with excitement. Yes, this was exactly what I wanted. I needed to know what it felt like to be possessed by a man like this.

He broke our kiss, lifted his head, smiled tightly, and then ripped my dress right down the middle. I hadn't been wearing a bra and my breasts popped free, my pink nipples hardened with anticipation. He threw one heavy leg over my thighs and then explored my body—cupping my breasts with one hand, dragging his fingers over their lush curves, fondling their nipples.

Filled now with only blind, hungry need, I ran my palms over the muscles in his broad back, then slipped them around his neck and tried to pull his head close, to demand another kiss. He refused me, though, and instead nuzzled the hollow of my throat, then left a trail of fiery kisses down toward my breasts. I stiffened with sheer delight when I felt his warm mouth close over one of my nipples and begin to suck. I laid there, passive, as he sucked one nipple and then nibbled at the pink tip. I let the burning heat wash through me, the sheer delight and a pleasure so intense it almost seemed to be more like pain.

He left off teasing my breasts and nuzzled the hollow of my throat, his fingers wandering lower, down to my abdomen, then past my belly button. When I instinctively tried to shield my pussy from him, he pushed my hands away and slipped one hand beneath my panties. He dug his fingers into the curls between my thighs, then spread my pussy lips and delicately teased that little bud of pleasure that swelled in response. The tremor of fire I felt when he touched me there made me arch against his exploring hand, and when he saw my unconsciously sensuous motion, an intent, urgent look crossed his face.

Abruptly, he shifted his body so that he was lying next to me. His movements quick and efficient, he pulled off his T-shirt, revealing that hard-muscled chest I'd seen in Beau Paradis. Seconds later, he'd rid himself of his jeans, too, and I caught my breath when I saw his cock, hard and far bigger than I remembered. It was glistening at the end with the evidence of his excitement. Shyly I touched that silky fluid with a fingertip, spreading it around the head of his cock, before reaching down and wrapping my palm around him.

He groaned with pleasure and kissed me, hard. But when I began to run my palm up and down his shaft—the same way I'd seen it done in the few porn movies I'd watched—he groaned even more loudly and shifted positions until he was on top of me. Bracing himself with his hands, he lifted himself slightly and slid a knee between my legs, then pushed higher until he'd parted my thighs.

I stared up into his heavy-lidded blue eyes, suddenly scared. The moment had arrived. I made a convulsive attempt to escape, twisting slightly away. With insistent hands he spread my legs wider. For an instant, he was poised above my trembling body; and then, with a savage thrust he entered me, his cock driving deep into my pussy.

Agony exploded through me. I screamed, the

sound lost as his lips claimed mine and kissed me hard. I hadn't been expecting pain like that. It felt like he'd driven a knife into my vitals.

He froze, an astonished look in his eyes. Clearly he'd felt that slight obstruction.

I wiggled a little, his cock like a hard, hot poker inside me. I could feel the head of it pressing against my womb. My earlier excitement had fizzled; now I felt nothing but pain. Tears filled my eyes and ran down either side of my face to the mattress.

He hesitated, uncertain. Obviously he couldn't take it back. And neither could I.

"I'm sorry, beautiful," he whispered. "Had I known, I would have been gentler. But you should have told me."

I turned my head aside, toward the mattress. I didn't want to look at him.

He leaned down and pressed a tender kiss against my temple, and then my ear, before trailing kisses down to my jaw line. Gently, lovingly, he coaxed me; and his kisses seemed to draw the very soul from my body. And yet, I still felt wounded, my insides throbbing.

Swallowing hard, I remained passive beneath him, and then he gave in to the demands of his body. He began to thrust and, even though his motions were gentle, the movement of his cock against that newly-torn membrane sent new jolts of pain through me. In less than a minute, he was thrusting faster, and groaning softly against me as his body tensed with what I knew to be an oncoming orgasm.

I felt his cock grow bigger, and harder; and fresh tears slipped down my face as he shuddered against me and then orgasmed, his cock spurting hot fluid deep inside me, the sensation unlike anything I'd imagined. He groaned some more and then collapsed against me, filling my senses, until I could see and smell and feel nothing but him. For a few minutes, he remained on top of me, balancing his weight with one knee so he wouldn't crush me, and then I felt him relax, his cock sliding out with a gush of fluid.

I immediately smelled a coppery scent and looked down to see blood on my thighs, and covering his cock.

He stroked my hair tenderly. "Why didn't you tell me?"

I drew in a hitching breath. My body still ached. An unsatisfied feeling gnawed at me. "I didn't think you'd want me if you knew."

"You should have trusted me." He gave a small sigh, and with gentle fingers, began to trace a circle around one of my nipples, which instantly hardened. "I'm very sorry for the way I...took you. Had I known you were a virgin, I would have made sure you had little pain."

"I wish I'd told you, too," I admitted. All of a sudden, I realized that the coolness, the remoteness which had been in his voice and manner earlier were gone. His blue eyes, which had previously looked like the coolest depths of the ocean, suddenly sparkled warmly, with an emotion I couldn't name. But my heart seemed to recognize it, because it leapt wildly in my chest, and made my insides tremble with excitement.

That wall between us, I thought, had come down—if only for a few moments.

He surprised me then by leaning forward and fastening his lips around one of my nipples. I let out a little gasp as his mouth left a little trail of fiery kisses from one nipple to the other, which he teasingly nibbled, and then moved hungrily up to my mouth. Unhurriedly, tenderly, he kissed me, until I forgot about the burning sensation in my pussy and relaxed into his arms, my mouth opening wide beneath his.

And yet, as soon as I started kissing him back, he stood up. He scooped me up against his chest, carried me into a bathroom, and put me in the shower. He turned on the water, adjusted the temperature, grabbed some sweet-smelling soap and washed me from head to toe. I relaxed with delight as the warm water sluiced over my abused body and his fingertips fondled me and coaxed every last bit of dirt and blood off of me.

When he was done, he helped me pile my wet hair loosely atop my head, put a white terrycloth robe on me, and led me back to the bed. He pulled the coverlet over the sheets to hide the blood stains, and told me to lay back down. Feeling wonderfully languorous, I did as he asked. He gathered two glasses and a bottle of champagne from a cabinet, opened the bottle and poured us both a glass. Then he sat down beside me and told me to drink.

I sipped, and we chatted about Beau Paradis and possible branding identities for the hotel. I thought it was funny that we were discussing business in the nude, right after he'd taken my virginity; and when I told him this, he laughed, too. Later, I mentioned the idea I'd had while taking photos: to bring a feel of old Hollywood glamour to the place, to give a sense of 1920's luxury and decadence, to pay homage to the long-dead stars who once considered Miami their playground. He loved it, and we talked a little more about ways we could achieve that goal.

He leaned back as he spoke and, after a time, he casually parted my robe, his gaze flicking over my breasts and between my thighs. I instantly remembered the pain I'd just experienced and compulsively moved away. He trapped me with his arms easily held me still, his eyes still sparkling with that wonderful, loving warmth. "Easy, beautiful. Once my mind is made up, I get what I want."

"But I'm still too sore—" I stuttered.

He cut me off by kissing me, his tongue plundering and exploring, while he leisurely explored my body with his free hand, seeming to want to memorize my curves, and discover what places on me evoked the most response. At first, not appreciating his high-handed attitude, I tried to deny the waves of pleasure that his touch brought, but his kiss was warm and demanding, and his caresses were experienced. It wasn't long before I gave in to him again, and parted lips wider, and slid my arms around his back to hug him closer.

Eagerly he pulled me against his hard, tanned body, his palms skimming over my back and bottom. I felt the coarseness of his chest hair against my nipples and the heat and hardness of his cock pressing against my thigh, and knew very well how this second encounter would end. Still, I wasn't a virgin any longer, and I continued to feel a tight ache that was both pleasure and pain, one only he could resolve.

Tentatively I touched him between his legs.

"Grasp it," he urged, his voice husky. "Feel it."

I reached down and closed my palm around him. His cock felt hard, and hot, with silken skin and a slight moistness on the tip.

He groaned deeply and his lips found mine again, and his hand roamed with increasing urgency down to my thighs. I was gripped by an intense desire to feel him inside me again, despite my soreness and pain; and I squirmed wildly beneath him, begging him without words to slide into me again, to possess me, to bring me to completion. And yet, despite my obvious desire, he continued to stroke me lazily, his fingers travelling downward to tease the little bud between my pussy lips again, caressing and fondling and stroking until a familiar tension gathered inside me and I thought I might scream if I didn't come soon.

He must have sensed this, for suddenly he shifted his weight until he hovered over me. I spread my thighs wide, and tensed only a little when the velvety tip of his cock nudged against my pussy.

"Easy," he murmured, and then slowly, gently, he slid into me. His mouth capturing mine and smothering my moans of ecstasy, he stretched me, filled me, and made the tension inside me worse; and then he was thrusting in and out, almost withdrawing completely before burying himself to the hilt inside me. His very first thrust brought a little pain, but each one afterward delivered only bliss. Every time he pushed in, his body pressed against my bud, and the bliss spread through me, growing and building until finally, I gasped and cried out.

A huge burst of pleasure exploded inside me, pleasure made more intense by the feeling of his hard cock, and I shuddered at the intensity of it, and the sheer joy and gratification it brought me. Seconds later, I felt his big body trembling with the force of his own release, and then he collapsed on top of me again, his breath warm against my cheek. After a few seconds, he rolled onto his side and gathered me close, his chin resting on the top of my head. He caressed my hip possessively and pressed a little kiss onto my hair.

I lay against him, stunned by the sensations he'd aroused in me. The warmth of his body penetrating mine felt so comforting, so perfect. I stretched so that his heart beat beneath my ear, almost in time with my own pulse; and then the sound of our heartbeats seemed to mingle until they became one. "Is it always like that?" I asked.

He stilled, and seemed to consider. Then, with a deep sigh, he whispered, "We have a connection, Demmie. I sensed it from the start. But I didn't realize...I didn't know..." he trailed off, unable or unwilling to express himself further.

I heard muted sadness in his voice, a strange kind of sorrow that was completely out of place, considering what had just transpired between us. A feeling of foreboding gripped me. "Is having a connection bad?"

He sighed again. "You asked about my first wife. She was a childhood friend. We married young, and after a few years, she had a miscarriage."

"I'm sorry," I said, unsure what that had to do with him and me.

"I loved her dearly." He toyed with a lock of hair that hung over my shoulder. "She killed herself two years ago."

"What?" I sat up and stared at him, my eyes wide.

"She didn't want to live any longer," he murmured, his voice wooden. "Money wasn't enough. I wasn't enough. So she killed herself."

"Oh my God, Jon, I'm so sorry." I touched his shoulder, wished I could comfort him in some way.

He shifted out of my reach and threw his legs over the edge of the bed. "I still think about her, but I don't long for her anymore." His voice sounded dismissive now. I realized that the wall he'd spoken of, the one he needed to place between us, was slowly going back up. "I'll never put myself in that vulnerable of a position again."

"That's why you only have sex," I breathed, suddenly understanding. "Why you never make love."

He smiled, but there was no humor in it. He stood, started pulling his jeans back on.

Another thought occurred to me. "You found out about my dad, didn't you?"

He shrugged his T-shirt on. "Your mom mentioned it."

"So you know he committed suicide about ten years ago?"

"It's one of the things that draws me to you," he admitted. "We have a shared grief. We can understand each other a little better than the world around us."

A sinking feeling gathered in the pit of my stomach. "You're drawn to me," I guessed, "but you won't let it go any farther than that."

"It would be better for both of us if I don't," he agreed.

I stood up and picked up my dress. It had a big rip down the front of it. It was ruined. I frowned.

[illegible]ed over to a drawer and pulled out a [illegible]it dress. He handed it to me. I held it [illegible]gers, as though it were poison. "Was this hers?"

"Yes."

"I don't want it, then."

"Don't be ridiculous," he chided. "You can't go home naked."

He had a point. I pulled it over my head, adjusted it down past my hips, then gazed at him with a challenging expression. "I look like her, don't I?"

"A little," he agreed.

"But I'm not her."

"Of course not." He walked over to me, tried to take me in his arms. I backed up a step.

"Oh, Demmie," he murmured, and when he approached me a second time, I let him put his arms around me.

"We didn't have sex, did we?" I asked.

"No. We made love. But it will never be more than this," he said, his voice cool. Remote. "Can you live with that?"

I scowled and tried to ignore the pain that was coursing through me...a heartache, this time. Still, I managed to lift my chin and nod sharply. "That's fine."

He released me, and looked at me closely. "You're sure?"

"Yes."

His lips curled in a half-smile, but I thought I saw a melancholy glint in his eyes. After one last, lingering look at me, he dropped his hands to his side and nodded toward the door. "Let's get you back to your hotel."

CHAPTER NINE

True to his word, Jon dropped me off at his hotel—he literally left me at the curb. Then, several days went by, several long days during which I took photographs and researched branding identities, before I saw him again. We met mid-morning, in the Barcelona's lobby.

"We're going to Beau Paradis this morning, Demmie," he said, as he approached me.

My camera in my hands, and the viewfinder displaying a photo of Beau Paradis I'd taken earlier, I looked up and drew in a breath. He appeared breathtakingly gorgeous as always, a perfect example of virility with his ruffled dark blonde hair, his deep blue eyes and the shadow of a beard darkening his square chin. Standing next to him, I realized anew how tall he was, and lean. His casual khaki pants, white long-sleeved shirt and Italian loafers emphasized that his leanness came with muscles, too, just where they needed to be.

I glanced at the gold hoop earring dangling from his ear and thought, not for the first time, pirate. Likely to plunder whichever woman interested him. A few weeks ago, that woman had been Vanessa, a bored Miami socialite whose accessories included two Olympic volleyball-playing boy toys. Later, that woman had been me. I thrilled inside at the memory of him ripping the dress off me, and kissing me until I couldn't think, and breaking that delicate little membrane inside me that had revealed me—somewhat embarrassingly--as a virgin.

The question was: Had he found a new woman? Or did he still want me in his bed?

He looked me up and down, a gleam in his eyes. "I see you went shopping."

I smoothed my dress down over my hips. I'd had time to spare over the last few days, so I'd picked up a few dresses, including the one I was wearing now: a khaki draped jersey dress, sleeveless, one that hugged my curves. I'd also bought two pairs of sandals, both with three-inch heels, which were by far the highest heels I'd ever owned.

"What do you think?" I asked, turning a little this way and that, aware that my breasts were pushing against the neckline and giving him a decent view of my cleavage. I was so happy to see him...every part of me was happy to see him.

"You look great." His gaze roved over to my breasts, and my nipples hardened as he stared at them, a little smile playing about his mouth.

My heart started to beat harder. "Thank you."

His attention switched to my camera. "You brought your Nikon. Good. I'm going to direct you, and I'll need you to take the photos."

A throb of excitement flickered through my veins. Our photo shoot on Key Biscayne had been a very sensual one. Would today include another? I smiled widely and gripped my camera. "Photos? That sounds wonderful! It would be my pleasure."

He lifted an eyebrow. "We're going to keep our

clothes on this time."

I choked back a disappointed sigh and quickly reminded myself that no matter what had happened previously, I still worked for him...I was his employee. "Of course, Jon." I glanced around. "Should I be calling you Mr. Baxter while we're working?"

His lips quirked in a smile. "You're trying very hard to please me today."

I returned his smile self-consciously. "I want to you to be happy with my...work. You're my boss, after all."

He looked at me from beneath suddenly heavy lids. "We did get off to a fairly shaky start. But you've been very...sweet since then."

I felt my cheeks grow warm as I remembered that towards the end of our first 'date,' he'd found out that I'd taken secret photos of him having sex with Vanessa in Beau Paradis. He'd spanked me for not only taking them, but also for not coming clean to him later. "I want things to go well between us. Really well," I replied fervently.

"Hmmm. Maybe I should test how far this newfound obedience of yours goes."

I recalled my visit to his house on Key Biscayne, and the way he'd so expertly teased and possessed every square inch of my body; and the subtle longing I was feeling for him blossomed into a honeyed ache. I lowered my lashes so he wouldn't see how intensely I wanted him. "I don't think you'll be disappointed."

He laughed aloud at my answer, and nodded toward the double doors that led outside. "Let's go."

I followed him through the lobby. He seemed in a good mood today, I thought, but I still sensed that cool remoteness in him, the one that had been between us ever since we'd left his home on Key Biscayne. I swallowed back my disappointment—I missed the warmth he'd shown me after we'd made love, that easy intimacy, that sense that I was someone very special to him.

We walked outside. Two bodyguards stood near the curb, their faces averted from us and scanning the street in front of the hotel, instead. A limousine was parked a little further back. As we approached the limo, Carlos climbed out and circled around to open the door for us. We both slipped into the limo and sat back as he shut the door. I glanced discreetly around, startled by all of the luxury around me, but determined not to look like a gawking middle-class working slob.

"Ever been in a limo before?" he asked, as we settled in.

"For my cousin's wedding. We had a stretch Hummer. But it didn't look anything like this."

I sat in a gray leather bucket seat that faced Jon's. A console between my seat and the empty one next to me had a flat screen console that displayed a map of the world and a number of glowing points on it. A scrolling newsfeed along the bottom of the display quoted stock prices. I noticed drink holders, reading lamps, magazine pouches, a trash chute, mirrors, tissues, a mini refrigerator, a wet bar... The console also offered a number of buttons, for heating the seats, for activating a massaging option, for adjusting the seatback, and others which I couldn't decipher.

Tentatively I pressed one, and another flat-screen TV lowered itself slowly from the car's ceiling. "It's amazing. You could live in this thing."

"It's my mobile office," he said with a little smile.

Clearly I'd amused him.

The car rolled away from the curb and started down Ocean Drive, toward the bridge that would take us from South Beach and onto the mainland. I returned the TV to the ceiling, relaxed back against the leather seat and tried to appear cool and sophisticated. "So, Jon, are you still interested in the branding identity we talked about yesterday? The one that equates Beau Paradis with old Hollywood glamour?"

He stretched his legs out and relaxed, too. My stomach did a little flip as I noticed how his tall, muscular body seemed to fill the inside of the limousine. I could smell his woodsy cologne, very faint but intriguing; and was acutely aware of the sexuality he exuded from every pore, one so potent it seemed to envelope me like an aura. His eyelids drooped, half-shrouding those magnetic blue eyes. "It needs some work, but it's a good start," he allowed. "Today, we'll take some test photos, and see how we can best create the impressions I'm interested in."

I nodded, and we continued to talk as the limo sped over to the mainland, then down south toward Coconut Grove. Before we reached the bridge that would take us to Key Biscayne, Carlos slowed, and we turned onto the metal and cement bridge that crossed Biscayne Bay to an oasis of green. The rest of the drive to Beau Paradis was as I remembered it: streamers of triangular blue flags along either side of a dirt road, backhoes parked near large swathes of cleared land, bungalows, a spa and tennis courts under construction, and then of course the hotel itself.

I saw that considerable work had been done on

the hotel since I'd been there last. It still appeared to be a combination of old, crumbling cement and new steel girders, but this time there were more girders than cement. The old section already had a roof, and the new section appeared to be completed.

The limo pulled up near the oceanfront entrance, with its large patio that had gone to weed. I few peacocks and peahens were wandering around the crumbling stones, but they ran away as Carlos parked the limo. I blushed as I recalled how I'd lied to Jon about seeing peacocks, when actually what I'd seen was him having sex with Vanessa.

Jon gave me a slightly mocking smile, and then gestured for me to precede him out of the limo. We got out and walked across the patio, with me taking photos as he directed. I took some of my own, too, if something struck me as worthy: a peacock hiding among a group of palms, with the blue Atlantic in the background; and the beautiful art-deco stained glass design that surrounded the old hotel's entrance.

After a while, we moved inside, and once again I stood in that cathedral-like lobby with its exposed water pipes and crumbling ceiling. I took photos of the art-deco mosaics hidden by years of grime, the arched walls, and that gleaming border of thin marble along the top of the wall, lit by sunlight. We shuffled through dried leaves and branches and construction garbage, our feet exposing the beautiful, finely-veined pink marble beneath.

At one point, Jon stood beneath the skylight that had caved in, and sunlight streamed down upon him like a benediction. It shone on his dark blond hair, burnishing it with gold, and painted his chiseled features with shadows and light. He looked like a

Greek statue sculpted by DaVinci himself, and my heart skipped a beat. I snapped a couple of quick photos, just for me.

"It's going to be magnificent when it's done," he said, and moved toward the grand staircase, which I had once imagined women in sequined gowns and men in tuxedos climbing to attend a soirée on the second floor.

I followed him and we both began the climb upward. My thoughts went back to the day I'd seen him having sex with Vanessa. "Did you know I was watching you that day?"

He paused, glanced back at me, then continued up the steps. "I saw you walking across the grounds, from the construction tent."

I froze for a second, one foot on the step above. "You saw me?"

"Yes." He reached the second floor and started down the hallway.

"And you knew I walked into the hotel?"

"I heard the doves fly away. You scared them."

I quickly ran up the final few stairs. "But you still had sex with Vanessa, even though you knew I was wandering around in the hotel?"

"Vanessa likes to be watched," he replied, his voice mild. "And I wasn't about to let a new employee spoil my day."

We got to the end of the hallway, then turned around and walked back. I took a few photos for good measure, but I was more focused on him than anything else. "So you knew there was a good chance I'd see you having sex with Vanessa, but you didn't care."

We started up another staircase. "I didn't think

you'd spy on me," he replied. "That surprised me. And then, later, when you didn't admit it to me, that surprised me even more."

I hung my head a little.

"From what Nat had said," he continued, "you're a 'good' girl, sheltered, with country ways. You spend your summers near the beach, catching crabs for dinner; or at the family farm, picking blueberries. During the winter, its snowshoes and hot cocoa for you. And the worst thing you've ever done is stay out past midnight."

I winced at the picture he was painting. "You make me sound like a banjo-picking backwoods hayseed."

He laughed. "Not at all. You're just...fresh. Genuine."

"Great," I muttered, thinking of Vanessa's high style.

"So, given all this wholesomeness, I just couldn't figure out why you'd hang around to watch me and Vanessa...and even take pictures to boot."

I shrugged. I was becoming acutely uncomfortable with this discussion.

He stopped and turned around. I heard a trickle of water and saw it pouring down from a broken pipe in the ceiling. I'd been following him blindly, and all of a sudden, I realized he'd brought me to the very place he and Vanessa had gone at it.

I frowned. "I was shocked. Startled. Seeing you and her...it made me feel strange."

"Excited?"

"Very."

He rubbed a hand across his chin, studied me for a moment. "I understand a little better now, of course."

"Just because I was a virgin, that doesn't mean that I was completely in the dark about sex," I countered.

"Oh, really?"

"Yes, really," I replied, my chin lifted.

"So why did you take those pictures, then?"

I thought for a moment, then lifted an eyebrow as I answered. "Because I'd never seen anything as decadent, as primal...or as beautiful."

We stared at each other for a moment. I saw that the wall between us was firmly in place. He wasn't going to allow himself to be vulnerable. "Why do I get the feeling that if I tried to hug you, you'd push me away?"

"Give it a try."

I walked slowly toward him, feeling desperate, feeling exposed, and wishing for something that I knew wouldn't happen. When I came close enough, I put my arms around him and hugged him awkwardly. His body felt like wood beneath mine. He turned his head away. I released him, my desperation now tinged with grief.

"There's a wall between us," I said.

He shrugged. "It's me, not you. I've already explained why."

I knotted my hands together, in an effort to keep that grief inside. "I know your wife wounded you. I know you've hidden your heart away because of it. But I'm not like her. I'm different."

"Demmie, don't fall in love with me," he said suddenly. "You're only going to get hurt."

I sucked in a little gasp of air. All at once, I realized that his warning had come too late. I was already in love...and I was already hurting, too. But I knew I couldn't let him see this. He wanted that wall between us.

And so I simply lifted an eyebrow and smiled seductively. "So...you don't like hugs. Do you like...blowjobs?" I almost choked on the word blowjobs as I said it, but managed to get it out nevertheless. I was eager for any kind of intimacy between us, even if it was just physical. And besides that, I wondered if physical intimacy could bring down the wall, if only for a little while—as it had last time.

A gleam entered his eyes. "Did you just ask me if I wanted a blowjob?"

I nodded and waited, unable to speak.

"Have you ever given a blowjob before?"

"Of course." The lie shot right out of my mouth this time. I helplessly glanced down at his pants zipper.

He lifted his eyebrows, as if he didn't believe me, but smiled nevertheless. "Make sure you lick it from the head to my balls. I like that."

At his words, my nipples hardened and my pussy clenched. I'd never had a cock in my mouth before. Jon Baxter had become a series of firsts for me.

His gaze on my face, he grasped his zipper and slowly drew it down. I watched, fascinated, as he reached into his pants and pulled out his fully-aroused erection.

I couldn't suppress a tiny gasp. His cock was big, just as I remembered. And thick. At the moment it was as hard as a rock, with a little bead of moisture at the top of its velvety head. I stared at it and wondered how I was going to get it into my mouth. Shocked by my need to suck on it and lick it—I moved between his legs and got down on my knees.

He wrapped his hand around its shaft and stroked it a little, then held it out to me, pointing it at my mouth. "Go ahead, Demmie. Show me what you've got."

Barely able to breathe, I leaned forward and gently kissed his balls. They smelled salty, musky, like Jon...but intensely so. I discovered that I liked the smell of him, and the taste of his skin against my tongue.

Not entirely sure what I was doing, I licked him from his balls, up his shaft like he'd asked. I'd seen a few porn movies and, remember that the women never broke eye contact with the men, I kept my gaze locked with his as I dragged my tongue to the top of his cock with a long, slow motion. His lower lips pouted, and he watched me intently, and I discovered then that while I liked the smell and taste of him, I absolutely loved teasing him like this.

Once I reached the tip of his cock, I circled my tongue around the head, from the back to the tip and then around again. His scent strong in my nose, and his cock like warmed velvet against my tongue, I teased out the little bit of moisture on its head so that I could taste him some more. Then I closed my eyes slowly, the sensations of the moment nearly overwhelming me.

He moaned.

I opened my eyes and saw that he continued to watch my every move. A smile of deep pleasure softened his face and eyes had grown dark with desire.

The wall between us, I thought with a triumphant little jolt, was down again.

My own excitement mounting, I wrapped one hand around the bottom of his thick shaft and slowly swirled my tongue around the mushroom-shaped head of his erection once more, and then licked the length of it again. The salty taste and musky smell and silky feel of his cock was incredibly pleasing to me, just because it was him; and I drew the motion out, as if I were licking a cherry-vanilla ice cream cone and wanted to taste every nuance of flavor. Yeah, I hadn't given even a single blowjob before, but this wasn't rocket science, and as I went along, ideas on what to do seemed to come naturally to me.

I loved sucking his cock, as embarrassing as it was to admit.

The next time I slid my tongue up to the head, I circled the tip of my tongue around it and under, pausing to give him a devilish smile as I gently flicked my tongue around it, then gently sucked on that small hole at the top. At the same time, the cleft between my thighs became open and wet and more-than-ready for him. The knowledge that he likely wouldn't satisfy me that way almost made me groan aloud.

I pulled him from my mouth and looked up at him, ready to ask him to make love to me.

"Nicely done," he breathed, before I could say a word. "Now finish it."

I held his cock loosely in my palm and saw more moisture glistening on the head. I took a moment to lick it off, then slowly slid my hand up and down his long, thick shaft. When he began to groan again, and he buried his fingers in hair, I went back to sucking him. My pussy aching, I licked him again, and again, drawing my tongue from his balls, up his shaft to the head, and then to the top of his cock, which glistened with moisture. I either licked the head or circled my tongue around it in a way that I knew he liked, judging by the look in his eyes and his small, almost unwilling groans of pleasure; and tried to ignore how my pussy quivered for his touch, for his attention.

Startled by how hot he was making me, just by being in my mouth, I sucked him for a good while, then circled my lips around his head and drew him fully past my lips. I swirled my tongue around the top of his cock, then began licking it harder, quicker, with full strokes from his balls to the head, then several smaller, faster licks around the head of his cock and against a spot on the underside that appeared to give him the greatest pleasure. I looked up at him the entire time, making sure I could see every little nuance of feeling in his face—this was the only way I could learn what he liked best. His eyes heavy-lidded, he placed a gentle hand on my head and dug his fingers deeper into my hair, caressing me even as his cock dripped with pre-cum.

"Play with yourself if you want," he told me, his voice a raspy purr.

Immediately I slid my hand beneath my skirt. I pulled my panties aside and began to stroke my bud as I sucked him. I was already hot and ready for him and, as soon as I touched that sensitive nub of flesh between my thighs, I felt an intense, pleasurable pressure begin to build. I licked him harder, using my tongue to tease him and taste him and bring him closer to an orgasm even as I felt my own body tensing up and on the edge of ecstasy. I was spinning, whirling inside a delirious void of sensations, my entire world filled up with him.

"Oh, Demmie," he whispered, his face tightening.

"So lucky to have found you—"

Abruptly, his cock grew very hard and grew bigger—something I hadn't realized possible. Then, without warning, an explosion of heat filled my mouth as he slumped forward, shuddering. I kept fondling the bud between my legs, but faster and harder now, even as he pumped more salty, bitter fluid into my mouth; and then, the sensations inside of me exploded inside with shattering force, even as I gulped his cum down. I didn't care, didn't care at all that I'd orgasmed while swallowing. Rather, I wrapped my arms around him and held onto him and pressed my hot face against his cock.

After a moment, he grabbed my arm and helped me to my feet. I wobbled a little, but then he wrapped his arms around me and held me tight. I felt his breath brushing against the hair at my temples. Tenderly he kissed my forehead. "You have this way...this way of sneaking beneath my defenses."

I had no words for him in reply. Instead, I snuggled against him, feeling secure in the circle of his arms.

He kissed me one more time, and then gently separated us be a few feet. "We should go back," he said, as he pushed his cock back into his pants.

I stood there, feeling bereft without his warmth. Tears formed in my eyes. "How did I do?" I asked with a mocking kind of confidence. "As good as Vanessa?"

He paused in pulling his zipper up and stared at me. "Don't say that."

"Why not?" I dashed the tears from my eyes and faced him with my chin lifted, and the salty taste of him strong on my tongue. "Doesn't Vanessa give you blowjobs?"

"You're nothing like Vanessa." He finished pulling his zipper up and regarded me with a deep frown.

"But you treat me like her."

"No, I don't. And you're going to stop acting like her."

"Why should I?"

He sighed. "You said that you were fine with 'just sex.'"

"I am," I quickly insisted.

"Then why this?" He wiped at the tears on my cheeks.

"Because it feels like more than 'just sex,'" I told him in a small voice, then grabbed his hand and pressed his palm against my heart. "My heart is like this whenever I'm with you. It beats so hard, I can barely breathe."

He sighed again, more deeply this time, and dropped his hand to his side. "You're so beautiful, Demmie. So sweet, and so innocent. I don't know what to do with you."

Why not just love me? I wanted to ask him. Still, I bit the words back and fixed my gaze miserably on the floor. Love was a word he'd refuse to hear.

He put a gentle hand on my chin and forced me to meet his gaze. He was holding, between two fingers, the silver ring he normally wore on his index finger. "This is for you."

My lips parted. I stared at it.

He grasped my right hand and slid the ring onto my right thumb. "Please wear it."

"What does it mean?" I held my thumb up, studied it. I wasn't sure how to feel.

"My tutor gave it to me, many years ago. I want

you to have it."

"So it's a friendship ring?" I started to slide it off my finger.

"Leave it on, Demmie," he said. "Don't take it off again."

I stopped, pushed it back.

He looked down at the ring and smiled. Seconds later his attention returned to my face.

I gazed at him, feeling off-balance, out of sorts, with fresh tears in my eyes.

His smile faded. Some intense emotion tightened his jaw. His eyebrows lowered slightly, and an unnamable feeling flickered in his eyes. He didn't blink, he just gazed at me, his full lower lip taut.

Another tear ran down my cheek.

He took a little breath and moved backward a tiny bit. Something about his manner told me he felt frightened. But then he stilled. He stared at me again. His face changed in a way I couldn't explain. And then, my heart skipped a beat, because for one brief moment, I could have sworn I saw a glimmer of hope in his eyes.

CHAPTER TEN

Two weeks later, I was asking myself, had I really seen hope in Jon's eyes? Or was it just a trick of the light? Because after we spent that morning together in Beau Paradis, he disappeared with a lame excuse about other business to take care of. I managed to get a few terse replies on the emails I sent to him, but otherwise, nothing. I assumed he had left Miami to take care of this 'other business,' whatever it was.

Of course, I had plenty of work to do, plenty of things to keep me busy. Natalie called a few times, and worked with me on the 'old Hollywood glamour' identity that Jon had given the preliminary go-ahead on. I made a few more trips out to Beau Paradis, to gather more ideas on how to improve upon the branding identity I'd come up with. At Natalie's request, I also worked with the interior designer Jon had hired for the hotel, to make sure we played up the glamour aspect inside as well. On the whole, the hotel's construction was coming along at a rapid pace. It looked like we were going to meet Natalie's one month deadline, which would place opening day right around Cinco de Mayo.

And yet, as tired as I was when I went to sleep at night, I still spent several restless hours tossing and turning, thinking about him. I remembered telling him about my ideas on the new branding identity, and how his broad, handsome face had become so serious as he'd listened them. I recalled him standing in Beau Paradis with me, his body superbly hewn, radiating masculinity, and seeming to draw the sunlight to him. I tried to forget that brief flash of sadness in his eyes when he'd told me he could never love me, that it would only be sex between us.

These thoughts, they tortured me, until I thought I would cry with frustration. But the worst of it was the loneliness I felt without him around, the relentless longing deep inside for his touch, the visceral memory of his cock buried deep inside me, impaling me, possessing me, thrilling me. It all came to a head the day before Natalie returned to Miami, when I talked to her on the phone as I was getting ready for dinner. She asked me if Jon had been taking good care of me.

"Good care of me?" I said into the phone. "I'm afraid I haven't seen Jon."

"What? Haven't seen him?" she yelled, her voice tinny through my cell phone's speaker. I heard a few muttered curses before she continued, "I'm gonna kill him. He was supposed to keep an eye on you until I returned."

I swallowed hard against a sudden knot in my throat and twisted the silver ring he'd given me on my finger. Yes, I still wore the ring, idiot that I was. "He's made sure I have what I need to work on the branding identity."

She fell quiet for a moment. I could almost see her considering—tilting her head, rubbing her chin. "I never asked you...how did your date with Jon go?"

I hesitated a moment before answering. "It went fine, even though you didn't tell me I'd be meeting the owner of the company."

She laughed, and then made a dismissive sound. "Would you have gone if you'd known you'd be spending the night with billionaire Jon Baxter, also my brother?"

"Probably not," I admitted. "I would have been too nervous."

"Well, there you have it," she said, with good cheer. "What do you think of him?"

"He's a...strange man," I managed, my heart clenching anew with a sense of loss.

"Did he take a shine to you?" she asked.

"Take a shine to me?" I frowned. "I'm not sure what you mean."

"Oh, never mind," she said, with her usual ebullience. "We'll talk more when I get back. My flight gets in at noon tomorrow."

"Do you want me to pick you up?" I asked.

"Not necessarily, darling, but thank you. Jon's in Miami, he can fetch me, if Carlos is unavailable."

I gripped my phone more tightly. Jon was in Miami? His long disappearance had led me to believe he'd left for parts unknown. "Okay. I'll be here if you need me."

We hung up then, and I slowly put my cell phone down. He was here, in Miami, but he was deliberately avoiding me. Or he just didn't care about me anymore. I choked back a sob. Either way, he'd abandoned me after fucking me and warning me not to fall in love with him. I should have never gotten involved with him, I should have never let him get to me the way he had...

Suddenly, the idea of going down to the Barcelona's restaurant to have dinner by myself—just as I'd been doing for the last several days—seemed intolerable to me. I walked over to my closet and pushed aside, one by one, the dresses I'd bought with the hopes of wearing them for Jon. When I touched a black silk one, a slinky knee-high dress with spaghetti straps and a low neckline, I paused. The dress was so fluid and revealing, it reminded me of a negligee.

I pulled it out of the closet, along with a pair of strappy high heels.

I wasn't going to have dinner by myself tonight.

I showered, then sat in front of the mirror, naked. I looked at myself, at the breasts he'd caressed, at the long hollow of my throat that he'd painted with kisses, and felt another throb of grief shiver through me. I ignored it and painted my lips with red lipstick until they were full, moist and inviting. I dragged the little stopper from my perfume bottle down my throat and around my nipples, leaving the scent of flowers on my skin. I shaded my eyelids with eye shadow that emphasized my blue eyes, and darkened my lashes with several coats of mascara, and put blush on my cheeks. I sprayed frizz tamer on my hair until my curls were soft and silky, and hung half way down my back in a molten chocolate mass. I put some makeup into a little golden evening bag I'd bought, and slung the bag around my shoulder. And finally, I took off his silver ring and put it in a little silk pouch, which I shoved deep into my luggage.

Silently, I swore that I wouldn't wear it again—not until the wall between us had come down for good.

The taxi dropped me off in front of the alley I'd visited before with Jon, although today, the area had none of the carnival-like atmosphere I'd seen previously. Instead, it was just a cobblestoned drive flanked on either side by homes, some of them well-to-do, and others not so much. I walked down the alley, my high heels clicking against the stone, and turned down the second alley to the restaurant that he'd taken me to that first night.

A different hostess than before stood outside the restaurant. Dressed in a colorful, gauzy dress; and with an orchid in her hair, she smiled as I approached and asked for my name.

"Demmie O'Reilly," I told her.

She glanced in an open book that sat atop a nearby dais. "I'm sorry, Ms. O'Reilly, but I don't seem to have a reservation in your name—"

"Of course Ms. O'Reilly may come in," someone said, cutting the hostess off, and I looked into the face of the woman who had attended to Jon and me during our previous visit.

I gave a little sigh of relief.

The hostess smiled graciously, and nodded, as the second woman took my arm and assisted my up the stairs. "Will you be joining us in the restaurant tonight, Ms. O'Reilly?" she asked, as we climbed toward the display of parrots.

"I'm not sure," I replied, realizing I should have thought the evening through a little more.

We paused on the landing to admire the parrots, which hopped from branch to branch. One of them squawked the warning I had heard it say before: be careful. I smiled. If only I had listened to it that first night.

"They're very beautiful," I observed.

"Ah, we love them so." She released my arm and gestured to a set of stairs leading downward. "Why don't I find you a seat at the bar, until you've decided you're ready to eat?"

I glanced down into the area she'd pointed to. The bar, like the restaurant, was situated in what looked like a grotto, with stone columns, ferns growing from the walls and waterfalls flowing freely from the ceiling. A granite-topped bar with bar stools hugged the back wall, while bar-height tables took up the rest of the available space. Throughout the room, couples and singles milled about, all of them in cocktail dresses, well-tailored suits, or tuxedos. "That would be perfect."

We walked together down the stairs. I kept my chin up as I made my way through the crowd, and I felt the stares of several men settle speculatively on me. I wondered what they were thinking...what conclusions they were reaching about a woman who had entered the bar apparently without a date. One black-haired man in a tuxedo turned his head to follow me with his gaze as I passed him by. I thought I remembered him from the sex club, when I'd visited with Jon weeks back. Hadn't he been the one to kiss my exposed skin, and send me from the club at a run? I tried not to let that intimidate me and took a seat at the bar. The hostess told me to let her know when I was ready to be seated in the restaurant, patted my hand, and then left.

Orchids, flickering candles, and beautiful pink flowers with fluttery petals sat in front of me, along with a bar menu. I breathed in the flowers' sweet, delicate fragrance as I glanced through the menu, then ordered a glass of champagne from the bartender.

The bartender, a swarthy fellow with dark hair and even darker eyes, flashed me a smile. "Drinking alone tonight?"

A middle-aged blonde woman sitting a few seats away turned her head, as if to listen to our conversation.

Not appreciating her intrusion, I switched to Spanish. "I'm here in Miami on business. My boss returns tomorrow," I replied slowly, translating from English in my head as I spoke.

His eyebrows went up for a brief moment. "You are familiar with my language, I see."

"I don't get to speak it enough. It's always a delight to refresh my skills, by talking to someone who's known the language from birth."

"From this moment until you leave," he declared gallantly, "I will speak only Spanish." Then, with a flourish, he went to fill up my champagne glass.

I watched him, amused and feeling more at ease; when suddenly, I noticed someone take the seat next to me. I turned to see who it was, and locked gazes with the black-haired man who'd watched me approach the bar. He looked me up and down, his gaze assessing, and arrogant in some way, yet intense and appreciative as well.

"I saw you come in," he said in English. "I had to speak to you."

My heart beating harder, I stared at him. Tall and broad-shouldered with a lean, muscular build, he had glossy black hair, stunning gray eyes and attractive features. His nose looked Roman, his mouth full, his jaw strong. And yet, I thought he might be a bit too polished, a bit too sure of himself. His manner was both sophisticated and calculating and, with him, I knew I was way out of my league.

The bartender returned with my glass of champagne, and I automatically thanked him in Spanish. As I did so, I noticed that the black-haired man stilled slightly. Realizing I might get rid of my would-be companion by pretending I didn't know English, I quickly made a few more inane comments in Spanish to the bartender, who answered them likewise with a smile, before he moved off to serve another customer.

A few moments passed. Then the black-haired man leaned towards me. "My name is Lucien," he said, his deep gray eyes gleaming in the candlelight. "But you don't understand me, do you?"

Secretly glad he'd bought my little ruse, I glanced at him helplessly.

"That's too bad," he continued, "because if you did understand me, you'd know that I think you're very beautiful. You'd know how much I wanted you from that second I saw you weeks ago, in the club. Your skin, it was like velvet when I kissed it."

I toyed with my drink, took a sip, shot a nervous glance his way, kept up the play-acting.

Boldly he sized me up, his gaze traveling from my high heels to the top of my head, and lingering on my breasts, which were barely covered by my silky dress. "Women like you come in here all the time," he told me. "Some of them come from a wealthy background, and others make a study of it—fashion, grooming; and how to project intelligence, style and reliability. But every one of them, they're beautiful. And all of them make more than the top traders on Wall Street."

As I realized what he was saying, I grew still, and a flash of embarrassment went through me like a heat wave. He thought I was a paid escort!

He moved a little closer, until his breath was tickling my shoulder. I started to move away. But then I slanted a glance at him, and those dark, beautiful eyes of his kept me in my seat. I took a quick little breath, and tried to ignore the way my heart was pounding. Yes, I had feelings for Jon, but my pussy still tightened at the thought of kissing this man.

The bartender came over then, glanced at my companion, and raised his eyebrows. "Everything okay, miss?" he asked in Spanish.

I managed a smile and nod. "My companion is a legend in his own mind," I replied, likewise in Spanish, "but I think I can handle him."

The bartender chuckled and moved off to mix a few drinks.

Lucien moved closer to me, until his body was mere inches from mine—so close that I could feel the heat from his body. "If I like you, it'll be more than a night." He spoke slowly, and paused to gauge my reaction, even though he thought I couldn't understand English. "I'll set you up here, in a condo, one of the best in town. You'll have a balcony, a view of the ocean, your own private beach. And I'll visit you, and bring you gifts." He reached out, grabbed a piece of my dress between two fingers and rubbed his fingers together, testing the silk, assessing its softness. "Dresses. Jewelry. Perfume. Satin lingerie. Silk stockings. You'll want for nothing."

I shifted slightly away, pulling my dress from his grasp, and stared into my drink. My gut roiled with indignation at his offer. And yet, some other, more primal part of me tensed with excitement.

Lucien dug into his pocket, pulled out a wad of bills and flashed them at me. "I don't know what your price is, but I'll more than pay it. I have a private cabana outside. It is the last one on the right. Please join me there." His voice had a husky, caressing tone to it, and again, my body thrilled to the idea of being in his arms. And yet, at the same time, I bristled at the idea that he thought I would trade sex for money. I stared at him for a moment, caught between desire and outrage, and then stood up abruptly and backed away.

He smiled, clearly unperturbed by my rejection, and very deliberately placed the bills on the countertop.

I spun around and made my way through the bar, and back up to the landing with the parrots. The hostess met me there, a look of concern on her face.

"Everything is okay, miss?" she asked.

I paused. "Just looking for the ladies' room."

She smiled, her face relaxing. "Through the restaurant, to your left."

"Thank you." I turned and went down the other set of stairs, the one that descended into the restaurant. Almost automatically I glanced toward the table I had shared with Jon that last time I was here, and saw a dark-haired woman sitting there, alone.

Vanessa.

I wondered where her two boy toys, Nat and Jordy, were.

Deciding to stop by and say hello on my way out, I continued through the restaurant, then turned down a corridor which led to the restrooms. With a little indrawn breath, I went into the ladies' room and leaned against the sink, my heart still fluttering in my chest. He'd thought I was a paid escort...

I straightened and examined myself critically in the mirror. The woman staring back at me had a gaze that was unquestionably mature, the blue eyes dark, and filled with a touch of longing. I blinked. For the first time, I realized exactly how far I'd come from the Maine country girl I used to be. My dress was truly spectacular, the silk molding itself fluidly to my curves, the neckline cut daringly low and revealing the sides of my breasts. My hair spilled around my shoulders and back, the curls gleaming with highlights. Two pale spots of color gave my cheeks a rosy blush, and my skin appeared flawlessly creamy.

I gave myself a wry, mocking smile. I could see why Lucien had mistaken me for a woman of the streets. I saw an unfamiliar lushness about me, a yearning, and a defiant vulnerability that hinted at a woman on her own, without support but determined to succeed.

Another woman came in, and I began washing my hands. I couldn't seem to get them clean enough. And as I washed, I wondered what I should do with the rest of my evening. Did I dare go back to the bar and risk being propositioned again? Frowning, I finally dried my hands off and decided yes, I would go back to the bar, and to hell with any man who considered me anything but what I really was: a career woman who was kicking back for the night, before starting a new work day in the morning. Deliberately I avoided thinking about Jon, and touched up my makeup with the mascara and blush I'd brought in my evening bag.

And, as so often happened to me, the second I stopped thinking about him, I ran into him. I walked out of the ladies' room and there he was, standing near a window and talking on his cell phone. My heart gave a giant thump in my chest. Suddenly I couldn't breathe.

He saw me and his eyebrows shot up. He motioned toward me, asking me to wait a moment. I thought he'd never been more handsome, more dazzling than he was tonight in a tailored black tuxedo. Wondering what had brought him back here--to this thinly-veiled sex club—I took in his powerful male form, encased in a black jacket with a single button, the jacket's V revealing a stark white shirt with pleats, his sleeves exposing a band of shirt cuff fastened with a gold cufflink. His black trousers were just long enough to skim the tops of his Italian leather dress shoes. I silently speculated as to whether he was wearing suspenders, too—to keep his trouser waistband perfectly positioned during an evening of high-stakes gambling and deal-making. He'd brushed his dark blond hair back from his forehead and his ocean-blue eyes gleamed at me as he finished his phone call.

I waited, my focus drifting across his broad cheekbones and square chin, and jumped when he finally spoke.

"What are you doing here, Demmie?"

My eyes widened at the annoyed tone in his voice. My heart still pounding, I lifted my chin. I could barely find my voice, but somehow, I managed it. "I'm here to enjoy my evening. Nice to see you again, Jon."

He smiled, but also appeared distracted. "I'm

sorry if I've seemed unavailable these past few days. I've been trying to close a business deal." He tilted his head and looked at me more closely. "Is everything okay?"

At his apology, the hurt that had been festering inside me flipped to hope. "I thought you'd decided..." I trailed off and, at his quizzical look, tried again. "I mean, when I didn't hear from you, I thought that I'd done something to turn you off—"

Surprise flitted across his face. Then he smiled and shook his head. "Sometimes, business just gets in the way."

"I know," I cut in, falling over myself to explain further. "I'm not high maintenance, I swear it. I just—"

He took a step closer. "It's okay. I know you're not very—experienced."

I blushed at his veiled reminder that he'd taken my virginity, and heaved a sigh.

His smile fading, he studied me closely. "You look...unsettled."

I felt the heat of a gaze upon me, and glanced over my shoulder. Lucien stood there, leaning casually against the wall, a little smile on his handsome face. He pulled the wad of bills out of his pocket and waved them at me, then turned and walked away.

I spun back around to face Jon. "He wants me to go with him to a private cabana," I hissed, my indignation winning out over other, sexy feelings I didn't want to acknowledge.

Jon glanced quickly at Lucien's retreating form, then returned his focus to me. He didn't appear angry, as I'd hoped. In fact, he seemed completely unfazed that another man had just made a play for me. "You're a beautiful woman, Demmie. Beautiful and sexy. Are you surprised he wants you?"

"But he offered to pay me."

A half-smile curled his wide, pink mouth. "Are you insulted, that he wants you so much, he's willing to pay you for it?"

"But it's not right," I insisted, shaking my head no ever so slightly. "It's disrespectful." But even as I said these words, I realized that Jon hadn't offered to make an honest woman of me after fucking me. In fact, he'd been quite clear about the fact that he'd never allow himself to love me. He'd given me nothing but a good time. At least Lucien had offered to pay me--

"Is it disrespectful?" he asked.

I scowled, my insides sinking. More than ever, I felt adrift in a place that I didn't understand, among people who were so far different from me that they might have been from Mars. I looked down at the floor, and suddenly, I wanted to cry. A tear slipped down my cheek.

He wiped my tear away with his thumb. "Why did you come here, if you didn't want to play?"

Stung, I opened my mouth, prepared to justify my behavior even though he'd been absolutely correct—when suddenly, I couldn't think of a damned thing to say.

"I'm going to give my driver a call," he continued. "He'll be outside at the curb. I want you to go back to the hotel."

"But it's still early—"

"No arguing, Demmie. Go back to the hotel. I'll see you in the morning." His voice brooked no opposition.

"Jon?"

I turned to see Vanessa approaching us.

She reached Jon's side and link her arm possessively with his. "Can you try to put business aside for just a little while?" she asked, with a smile in my direction.

I froze inside, realizing now that he'd brought Vanessa here. They were having dinner together. He didn't have time for me, but he had time for her. Unreasoning fury filled me, along with a deep sense of betrayal. Goddamn him, for taking my virginity and then discarding me like a used condom!

"Thanks, but I don't need a ride back," I said to him, my lip curling.

Jon's face tensed. "Demmie..."

Vanessa lifted an eyebrow. "Am I intruding?"

"No, of course not," I grated. "You're not intruding at all. Now, if you'll excuse me--"

"Wait a minute," Jon cut in, a hint of anger entering his voice. "You're playing at a game you know nothing about."

"Oh, am I? I think you've done a pretty good job teaching me how to play."

"Play what?" Vanessa demanded.

His lips tightened. "Don't be an idiot—"

I didn't listen to any more. I simply spun around on my heel and stalked away. After I'd made it half way through the restaurant, I looked over my shoulder. He still stood there, frowning and looking at me, with Vanessa clinging to his arm.

The sight only added fuel to my fire.

I marched up to the bar where I'd sat earlier and demanded another drink from the bartender...this time, in English. A few moments later, he returned with it. His face expressionless, he also handed me a wad of folded up bills. "From Mr. Entrage," he said.

I took the money. My fingers trembling, I counted out one thousand dollars. I thought of Jon in the restaurant with Vanessa, finished my drink, and stood up. What was that old saying of my mom's? If it was good enough for the goose, it was good enough for the gander...

I shoved the bills into my little golden evening bag, and went in search of my newest admirer.

□

CHAPTER ELEVEN

My dress slid sensuously across my skin as I made my way out the door and into the club, which stretched far, far back...all the way to the beach. As before, couples lounged on white pillows atop rattan sofas and chairs. Others ordered drinks at bars, or accepted drinks from waitresses who roamed through the sand in bikinis, with trays balanced on their arms. Latin-style instrumental music filtered through unseen speakers.

I knew that the cabanas were situated at the very end of the club, and sat closest to the ocean. I walked down the stone path that weaved in and out of the patio area, before giving way to sand. Following the sound of waves crashing against the shore, I shucked off my high heels and passed through the sofas and chairs, and then white-draped beds and cabanas situated right in the sand. Torches provided the only illumination throughout the club and enabled both intimacy and anonymity. They painted shadows on the couples writhing on the beds, hiding their faces. I knew my identity would be hidden as well, once I found Lucien and gave him what he'd paid for.

A part of me wished that Jon would come after me. That he'd stop me from doing this thing, and thereby cheapening what he and I had known together. But when I risked a glance backward, I saw that no one was following me—that this decision would be mine, and mine alone.

I continued walking toward the ocean, the sound of the waves getting louder. Finally, I reached the end, and paused before a full moon that created a silvery trail on the water and painted the sand gray. Even though my insides still heaved with a sense of betrayal and an even more wicked anticipation, I had to stop and appreciate the beauty of it.

Fighting the need to have Jon with me, enjoying this moment, I looked to the left and right. Tent-like fabric cabanas facing the ocean stretched out on both sides. Some of them had lights glowing within, while others appeared empty. I walked toward the right, my feet sinking into cool sand, and redirected my gaze away from the cabanas I passed, for fear of witnessing someone's private moment. I kept going until I reached the last one. Sure enough, when I got there, I saw that the cabana housed a white-draped bed, along with a small sitting area and a private bar. Several candles which sat on a wicker coffee table provided the only light.

I stepped inside and looked around. Saw no sign of Lucien, and wondered what to do next. Should I sit there and wait for him? I found a wicker chair and sunk into it, reveling in the luxury in spite of my circumstances, and gazed out across the ocean.

Emotions stirred, and soon I was seeing another bedroom, and another couple. I had been wearing the white gauze dress that day, and our wild Jeep ride had ruffled his thick tawny hair, and he'd whispered so softly in my ear as his arms had enfolded me. He'd made me a woman and shown me the ecstasy that making love could bring. Now, I went over every detail of that encounter in my mind and mourned the loss of it. Jon not caring, Jon unable to love, leaving me alone in a world suddenly without meaning.

I swallowed against the knot in my throat and fought the tears back. I wasn't going to give in. I wasn't going to surrender to the depression that thoughts of Jon brought. I'd lived the last twenty-four years of my life without even being aware of Jon Baxter's existence, and I had every intention of getting over him and living the next fifty years free of the emotional turmoil he'd brought to me. My fists clenched, I took a deep breath and stared out across the ocean. This time, I thought, it would be sex. Never again would I allow my heart to become involved.

Almost immediately, I saw a dark shape moving close to the shore. A few seconds later, I realized that the dark shape was a man. I watched as he strode away from the waves and picked up a towel on the beach. He was still rubbing his hair when he approached the cabana. I swallowed at the sight of his muscular body, at the little droplets of sea water clinging to his skin. His bathing suit—a speedo—left nothing to the imagination.

"Ah, mi amour," he breathed, when he saw me.

Forget Jon, I told myself. Focus on the now. My pulse abruptly throbbing, I grimaced. "I speak English."

He paused for a second, then looked at me with admiration. "So you knew what I was saying the entire time."

I nodded.

He wrapped the towel around his waist. "You

received my offer?"

I took the wad of bills out of my evening bag and put it on a wicker chair.

"What is this?" he asked. "Are you turning me down?"

"I don't want your money."

"You must take it. It's more exciting that way. And I'm sure you'll earn it." He strode over to a cabinet, pulled out two glasses, and selected a bottle. "You like champagne?"

My conscience told me to get the hell out of there. Then I thought of Jon, eating dinner with Vanessa at the same table he'd taken me to. "Yes, I like champagne."

He popped the top on the bottle and, his back to me, he busied himself with making us drinks. When he was finished, I took the one he offered to me, and we both sipped. I nodded appreciatively. The champagne had a lovely licorice taste to it.

He remained standing, his glass in hand. "You look sad."

I shrugged. "I'm not."

A gently mocking smile curled his lips. "You stare at the bed. It reminds you of other times. I understand."

I assessed the leanness of his body, the strength of his partially-bared thighs and arms. He was strong and beautiful. His masculinity pulled at me and frightened me at the same time. "You're mistaken," I replied stiffly.

He lifted an eyebrow. "You feel empty inside. You have very strong needs. You try to deny them, but eventually, they boil up inside you. You need relief." His mocking smile widened. "I'm the same way."

I took a nervous sip of champagne and choked back a laugh over his flowery language.

"Relax," he murmured.

In the candlelight, his eyes looked very dark, and they seemed to gleam with compassion. They made me forget that he and I had made a deal, that I had already been paid for a service I had yet to deliver. This game that we were playing, it was just a nicety to make sex seem more like making love.

"Drink," he ordered with his Latin arrogance, and I obeyed. The champagne bubbled warmly in my stomach and it soothed me, comforted me. He moved nearer, and all at once, his smile appeared gentle rather than mocking.

"You've very beautiful. Very young." He toyed with a curl that had fallen against my shoulder. "How many men have you known?"

"I've known plenty."

"I don't think so." He sat down next to me, his thigh pressing hard against mine. I could see the outlines of his erection pushing up against the towel he'd wrapped around himself. "I think you're new to this game. New, and hungry."

"No," I whispered.

He held up one of his hands for me to look at, displayed long, sun-browned fingers and wide palms. "You want these fingers to stroke every inch of your body, and find all of your secrets. You want me to lay atop you, and crush you against me. You want me to slide into you as deep as I can, until all you can do is wiggle and squirm and clench around me."

I sucked in a quick, shallow breath. This time, I had no desire to laugh.

He smiled. "I thought so."

He was so strong, and so sexy, and he understood so much, that suddenly, thoughts of Jon were far away. A delicious weakness stole through me, and for just a second, I wanted to yield completely to his power. To become his one-night stand and to savor all of the pleasures he'd paid me to enjoy.

"Tell me that I'm right," he coaxed. "I want to hear you say it."

I nodded almost sleepily and held a hand out to him.

"Say it. Tell me you want me."

I let my hand drop to my lap, a flame of desire surging through my veins.

He smiled. "Do you like both women and men, or just men?"

Heat flushed through my body.

"Which is it?" His black-brown eyes insisted I submit.

"Just men," I admitted.

He chuckled softly. "So you prefer cock."

I lowered my lashes to hide the fact that I was on the verge of surrender, and sipped more champagne, aware that it was creating a far brighter fire in my belly than I'd experienced before. I glanced at my glass and noticed, for the first time, that the champagne had a slightly milky cast to it. "Are we drinking champagne?"

"Champagne and absinthe." He swirled the contents of his glass.

"Oh." I swirled the contents of my glass, too, and then sipped again. "It's very strong."

"One of the strongest," he agreed, and pressed the entire length of his thigh against mine.

The heat of his skin penetrated the thin silk of my dress. I could smell him, a male scent coupled with the salty scent of the ocean. Deep in the back of my thoughts, I heard my mother saying, you will not do this with him. Almost simultaneously, an image of Jon wavered in my head. I pushed it all away. The candlelight around me grew dim, and the rest of the cabana faded away, until there was nothing but this man next to me, this man with his hard body and sweet words and mesmerizing eyes.

"How do you like the drink?" He began toying with the curl on my shoulder again.

"It makes me tingle."

"It's wonderful, isn't it?"

"Yes," I admitted, my voice breathy. All at once, I realized I was feeling almost...drugged. Alarm bells were going off in my head. They were faint, though. Far away.

"It makes you feel free," he agreed. "To demand what you need."

"Yes."

"And right now, you need me inside you. It's easy. Just pull up your dress, and take your panties off. You're wearing panties, aren't you?"

He smiled--a sexy, wonderful smile—as he stood up and wandered over toward my evening bag. His attitude playful, he opened my bag and dropped the bills he'd given me earlier into it.

"I don't want your money—"

In a second, he was at my side and pressing a gentle finger against my lips. "Shhh."

I shifted around uncomfortably, suddenly aware of that constricting silk fabric blocking my skin from his. The drink he'd made me burned in my stomach, then turned into warmth that flowed through my veins, taking my inhibitions with it, making me forget the money. He raised one hand and set it gently on my shoulder; spread his fingers out and curled them into my skin, kneading and clenching until he slid his hand up to settle behind my neck and massage me there.

I sighed softly, the combination of his touch and the drink so pleasant, so numbing.

He chuckled, as if reveling in the control he had over me. His hand pressed against the back of my neck, and tightened, drawing me closer, then closer still, until his eyes were mere inches from mine and I could feel the warmth of his breath against my lips. Slowly, clearly savoring every moment, he bent his head toward mine until our lips grazed each other's. I felt the pressure of his mouth but didn't move away, for he'd cast some sort of spell over me, he'd left me powerless with his sweet words and drink.

And yet, with the touch of his lips, I fully realized what I was about to do. Abruptly, I didn't want him. I didn't want to do this. But my head was spinning, and I hadn't the strength to break free.

He lifted his head a fraction to look at me. I stared at him from beneath lowered lids, and then glanced around the cabana. Candles glowed, bathing the cabana's fabric walls with golden shadows. An oriental rug covered the sand, and that enormous bed sat off to one side, its mattress covered with white sheets. Leafy green plants with tight, waxy buds spilled from a vase atop the private bar, and two plush bean-bag chairs sat facing the ocean. It looked like the setting from a dream.

"Kiss me, you little slut," he breathed, his voice so quiet I barely heard him. "You're going to take my cock in your ass, every inch of it, and then I'll fuck your pussy."

I made a little shocked noise, but then his lips closed over mine once more. He held me in a firm grip, his fingers squeezing skin and flesh. I felt trapped, unable to stop him and, in that moment, the dream became a nightmare.

Somehow, I had to free myself from the silken web he'd woven around me. I pulled away a little, and his fingers kneaded the back of my neck, forcing me closer, his tongue jabbing boldly past my lips. I made a little trapped sound in my throat. The cabana walls seemed to close in on me. I had trouble breathing. My heart was beating furiously and pounding against my rib cage. I yanked my face aside and gasped.

"Relax," he crooned, his voice soothing. He reached down and captured my wrists, then held them behind me and twisted me slightly, pulling the silk dress aside to expose my left breast. It stood full and firm and milky white, tipped with a throbbing pink nipple that grew tight with excitement as he gazed down on it.

"Beautiful," he murmured, and released my hands. He leaned downward, wrapped his lips around my nipple and sucked vigorously, sending tendrils of fire through my veins. Involuntarily I arched my back, pushing my breast toward him, and he sucked harder, then squeezed one hand around my breast and gazed at the swollen nipple. "Little slut," he whispered.

I knew I was teetering on the edge. I was coming to the point of no return and fought savagely against the desire he'd aroused in me. I repeated to myself that this wasn't right. He'd drugged me somehow.

Given me something to drain me of my will. Dosed me with an aphrodisiac. I had to break free before something terrible took place.

Mustering the last of my strength, I reached up and wound my fingers into his hair, then yanked backwards. His head jerked back and he cried out. Without warning, he drew his hand back and slapped me sharply across the face. I let out a gasp and scrabbled away from him, shocked, my cheek burning, the desire now completely gone.

"You little bitch," he growled, "you owe me!" He surged forward, his erection swollen and hard beneath his Speedo, and lunged at me. He pushed on top of me and scrabbled at my dress, trying to get past the fabric barrier, his stiff member poking at me like a spear. I heaved and pushed and did my best to keep him off of me, scratching him and hissing like a cat, clamping my legs together and straining away from his lips, which plunged toward mine.

"What in hell is going on here?" a man's voice asked.

Lucien froze. I seized the opportunity and scrambled away from beneath him, then looked up at Jon, who stood on the sand outside the cabana. His blue eyes were stony, and there was a dangerous curl to his mouth. He was staring first at Lucien, and then at me.

I stood and smoothed my dress down. Readjusted my bodice. And fought a deep sense of shame.

Lucien stood up, adjusted his Speedo, and wrapped a towel around his waist. He gave Jon a sheepish smile.

Jon didn't return it.

Lucien shrugged and poured himself a fresh glass

of champagne. "The lady and I have business to conduct."

"Business?"

Lucien shrugged. "She's been paid well."

I sucked in an outraged breath. "I told you, I don't want your money!"

Lucien gave a very Gallic shrug, as if to say, women! "I offered. She accepted. I didn't know she was yours."

"She isn't," Jon retorted, and I thought I heard a little catch in his voice. He turned to me. "Get your things. We're leaving."

I nodded, scooped up my evening bag, and followed Jon out of the cabana.

□

CHAPTER TWELVE

Jon hustled me back up the path to the restaurant, earning a concerned look from the hostess along the way. When we passed the dining area, I snuck a glance towards the table where Vanessa had been sitting.

It was empty.

What had happened to Vanessa? I wanted to ask him, but he didn't give me the chance. His grip firm, he propelled me down the stairs and outside, to his limo, which waited at the curb. Carlos sat behind the steering wheel.

I climbed inside and slid across the leather seat. He stopped by Carlos, muttered "The Barcelona," and then climbed in himself. He sat on the seat opposite me and looked out the window.

The limo pulled forward, entered traffic, turned onto Ocean Drive. All around us, sports cars gunned their engines, tourists and locals crowded the sidewalks and clubs blared dance music into the night. Midnight had come and gone, but South Beach was just revving up.

"Jon, I know what it looked like," I started, my throat tight.

"What did it look like?" he quickly asked, as he swiveled to study me with cool blue eyes. "What do you think I saw?"

I shifted miserably on my seat. "I got in over my head. Didn't know what I was doing."

"I told you to go home."

"I felt lonely," I admitted. Fresh tears sprang to my eyes. "I couldn't spend another hour in my room alone. That guy, Lucien, he bought me a drink, had nothing but compliments for me—"

"And he had a stack of bills for you too, didn't he?" Jon's voice sounded frosty. "So you took them, in exchange for sex."

I swallowed. "I didn't take his money."

"That's not what he said."

"He's lying," I insisted.

Jon frowned. "What the hell were you doing there in the first place?"

"I didn't know where else to go," I stuttered.

"There are thousands of restaurants in Miami—"

"I just went with what I knew."

"And then, of all the men, you had to pick Lucien Entrage." Jon shook his head. "He's a player, Demmie. And he doesn't like to lose. He's got a spoon up his nose, a MAC-10 in the trunk of his Lamborghini and friends in every branch of the justice system. There've been a few women who've complained about him...but they've quickly shut up. Or disappeared."

I let out a shocked breath. "Jesus."

He gave me a tight smile. "That's right. So what happened? How did you two hook up?"

"He just...came over to the bar and sat next to me. At the time, even his company was better than sitting alone. I didn't know he was Satan in disguise."

"And then you made the brilliant decision to go to

his cabana with him."

I dashed my tears away and glared at him. "I wasn't thinking straight! He gave me this drink—"

"Champagne and absinthe," he stated flatly. "It's his signature."

"It made me really woozy," I continued. "I almost couldn't tell him no. But then...I came to my senses. I tried to fight him off. You saw," I added hopefully.

He ran a distracted hand through his hair. "Didn't I tell you that you're out of your league here? I thought you were smarter than that."

I scowled at him. "I know better now. As I said—I didn't know what I was doing. I felt lonely."

A few seconds of silence passed, during which he assessed me, his eyes still dark with anger. Suddenly, he narrowed them. "There's something that you and I need to get straight. I don't share my women with anyone. Do you understand? If you want him, then you and I are going to part ways now."

My eyes widened. Shock reverberated inside me. After his long absence, I'd thought he didn't give a goddamn. "You think I want that Lucien guy?"

He lifted an eyebrow. "Do you?"

"No way!"

"That's better."

A rush of unexpected joy made me feel light inside. Clearly he cared about me after all! I grasped his hands and held them in my own. "I'm so sorry."

"Don't betray me, Demmie," he said, his voice tight.

"I won't. But I don't want to share you, either."

"You're not sharing me," he replied.

"What about Vanessa?"

"You need to trust me."

I stared deep into his eyes, looking for a lie. I didn't find one. My joy grew. "Okay."

We fell silent then, and he continued to stare at me, his expression becoming pensive. Finally, he brushed the curls back from my face and pressed a kiss against my forehead. "You really scared the hell out of me. I thought I was going to kill Entrage."

I ran my fingers over the back of hand, tracing his knuckles with a light touch. I just wanted him to kiss me now. "I'm sorry. I am out of my league. I should have listened to you."

He slid an arm around my back and drew me close against him. "You'll listen to me from now on?"

"I promise."

He cupped my breast, then rubbed my nipple with his thumb. "Good answer."

I stretched against him, languidly, a bud of excitement unfurling inside. "I wouldn't want you to have to spank me again."

He chuckled and ran his hand down my abdomen, pausing to finger the silk hem of my dress. Slowly he drew the hem of my dress upward, exposing my panties. His breath felt warm against my neck. "We have about five minutes until we get back to the hotel."

I gulped, my pussy quivering with anticipation of his touch.

"Do you want me to fuck you, beautiful?" he asked.

My heart pounding, I glanced toward the front of the limo. "Will Carlos see?"

Smiling, Jon closed the curtain separating the front from the back seats. "Pull your panties down. Spread your legs. Show me."

Trembling, I hooked my fingers into my panties and slowly slid them down past my thighs. His gaze immediately dropped to my pussy, and I felt an answering throb down there, an almost unbearable eagerness. He reached down and pulled my panties the rest of the way off.

I spread my thighs and remained as still as I could, while he inspected my pussy, touching it with one finger, then parting my pussy lips to tease the little velvety opening between them, and the bud above.

"You're very wet," he observed.

My entire body afire for him, I reached forward and unsnapped his trousers waistband. With his chuckle in my ears, I yanked his trousers down, and then reached inside his boxer briefs. As soon as my hand closed around his cock, he groaned.

"That's it, beautiful." He leaned forward to kiss my forehead with warm, insistent pressure. "Show me what you want."

I nodded, wonderfully indolent now, and pushed the briefs down, freeing his cock. I wrapped my palm around it once more and led its hard, silken head to my pussy. He slipped the spaghetti straps from my shoulders, exposing my breasts, and then placed one hand next to my shoulder. With his free hand exploring my breast, he leaned down to claim my mouth with his own, his body covering mine completely. That magnificent ache spread through me as his lips parted and probed, his tongue slipping inside my mouth to tangle with mine; and then he straddled me. He shifted even closer, his knees resting on the limo's floor, his thighs lightly furred with blonde hair and tightening between mine. His tongue jabbed at the back of my throat and he went on kissing me, until my entire world became only him.

I teased the opening between my pussy lips with his cock, pushing him in a little and then pulling out again as his hand wrapped around my breast and squeezed, my nipple swelling against his palm, his mouth smothering my moans of ecstasy. He groaned loudly and, after only a few moments of my teasing, drove into me. I cried out at the delicious sensation of having the hard, hot length of him inside me, filling me, pushing all the way up to my womb.

I was spinning, whirling in a void of pleasure. I no longer heard the sports cars or the crowds of people outside the limo, and I didn't care about Vanessa. All I knew was the feel of his lips on mine, and the heat of his sweet, hard cock deep inside me. I gripped the sculpted muscles of his back and lifted my hips to meet each of his thrusts. Slowly, the void inside me expanded, grew emptier, and seemed to gather up before exploding inside with shattering force.

I moaned aloud with the strength of it, and felt a chuckle rumble through his chest as he, in perfect control, allowed himself the ultimate pleasure, now that I'd had mine. He thrust a few more times in quick succession, and then pulled out to orgasm all over my exposed breasts. Still caught in the intense pleasure, I eagerly rubbed his cum over breasts and nipples, reveling in the silken feel of it.

Just then, the limo stopped. Jon quickly sat back and shoved his cock back into his boxer briefs. I pulled my dress up, aware that it was sticking to the cum all over me. We both finished rearranging our clothing just as Carlos opened the door and invited to exit. Jon got out first, and then extended a hand to help me out, and kept me from falling over when my legs wavered. I guessed that the smell of sex coming from the limo had to be intense, but Carlos didn't even bat an eye as he closed the door and lingered nearby.

"Aren't you coming up?" I asked, as I eyed Carlos.

"I can't, beautiful. I'm sorry," he replied. "But I'll see you tomorrow. Nat's back. She said she'd meet you first thing in the morning."

I nodded, feeling off-balance. He'd fucked me, and now he was leaving me curbside like a piece of luggage. I suddenly felt very much taken for granted.

"Eight AM, in the lobby," he added, and then got back into the limo. I watched as the car drove away, its red tail lights combining with the other traffic on Ocean Drive, until it was undistinguishable.

It wasn't until I returned to my hotel room and emptied my evening bag, that I found Lucien Entrage's wadded up stack of hundreds, shoved deep inside.

"I read your branding proposal," Natalie said the next morning, as we sat together over a cup of coffee in the Barcelona's restaurant. "I think it's brilliant. I see you've already received Jon's approval, so I'm forwarding it to the marketing department this afternoon. We have about two weeks until the hotel opens, and we'll need every second between now and then, to make sure the world knows about it."

We had my 'Hollywood glamour' proposal spread out in front of us, and Natalie was sifting through the various photos I'd taken on my company iPad.

"Do you have any changes or additions to make?" I asked.

"One or two things, here and there. For the most part, I'm leaving it alone." She gathered her curly brown hair behind her neck, then pulled it up into a bun with an elastic band. "I forgot how uncomfortable it is here. The Riviera was hot, but Miami is absolutely hellish." Without much of a pause, she switched subjects. "Get your notepad out, Demmie. I'm going to give you the details of our opening day. When was the last time you were out there, by the way?"

I thought for a moment as I reached into my briefcase and brought out my laptop. "About a week ago. I've been working on the proposal since then."

"Have you lined up any promotional companies?"

"I sent out a request for proposal as soon as Jon gave me the okay. A few bids have come back, and one of them is very reasonable." I opened the laptop and started a new document.

"Forward it to me."

We paused as a waitress brought over our breakfast orders—a small bowl of fruit for me, and a croissant for Natalie. I took the opportunity to draw in a few deep breaths. Like before in Natalie's presence, I felt like I'd been caught up in a small hurricane--she was a whirlwind of thought and activity.

"We're going to offer our best clients fifteen percent off our best rates," she said, once the waitress had gone. "We're also going to hold a Cinco de Mayo grand-opening gala."

"I noticed we've been advertising," I said, my fingers typing away on the laptop.

"For months now," she confirmed. "Since this is Miami, I've chosen a Latin theme for the gala. It'll be based both inside the hotel and outside on the patio, with music and entertainment. And gourmet dining, of course."

She gave me a few more details on what she'd already arranged, and I made some notes about additional things I needed to accomplish. Her enthusiasm was infectious, and as we went back and forth like this for another five minutes, I started to feel very excited about the launch.

"What I haven't yet figured out is how to incorporate the old Hollywood glamour theme," she admitted over a bite of croissant. "I'll leave that up to you."

"But the party is only two weeks away—"

She smiled brightly. "Surely you can arrange something. Who needs sleep, anyway?"

I had to return her smile...I couldn't help it. "I'll do my best."

"I know you will, darling." She eyed my bowl of fruit. "Enough note-taking for now. Eat your breakfast."

I obediently saved the document and put my laptop away. But as soon as picked up my fork, Jon stepped into the restaurant and walked toward us. He was wearing brown Italian loafers, wheat-colored trousers and a loose linen shirt. His tawny hair was brushed back from his forehead and glimmered in the sunlight that slanted through the windows. Shadows stretched across the diners around us, but they didn't seem to touch him.

He stopped next to our table.

Natalie eyed him up, then grinned. "Mr. Baxter."

Jon smiled and shook his head. "Glad you made it back okay. I take it Nick couldn't do without you?"

"He needed me, and he knew it. At least he's willing to admit it." She waved to a third chair at the table. "Sit down. We're just talking business."

His warm blue gaze lingered on me, and a smile turned his lips upward. He didn't seem to have heard her.

I shyly returned his smile.

Natalie sat back in her chair. "Oh, now that's interesting."

Clearly distracted, he turned toward her and lifted an eyebrow. "What's interesting?"

"Nothing." She gave him a mysterious little grin. "Are you going to sit down, Jon?"

"I'd like to, but I have a meeting over at the docks." His gaze caught mine again and held it for a few seconds more before focusing on Natalie. "Just wanted to make sure you two ladies didn't need anything before I left."

"I don't think we need you." She slanted a curious look toward me. "What do you think Demmie? Do we need him?"

"It's nice to have him around," I offered playfully, my throat catching at the handsome picture he made. He stood in a pool of sunlight with his arms folded across his chest, and seemed as solid and strong as solid granite. "But if he has something better to do—"

He groaned. "You two are tough broads. I'll be back later. Call me if you need me." He turned on his heel and left, with Natalie's "Will do" aimed at his back.

She watched him go, her gaze assessing. A few

moments passed, during which she toyed with her croissant. Then she fixed me with a penetrating stare. "Tell me, Demmie. Did Jon keep an eye on you while I was gone? Did he help you adjust to working at B3?"

I blushed and looked down at my bowl of fruit. "He did, although he was gone for a while, too."

"Ah, yes, I know. I yelled at him for that, but there was no getting around it. He had to go back home. Our dad was in the hospital, and Nick couldn't get away from the Riviera."

"Your dad's better?" I asked, suddenly feeling guilty about all the angst I'd felt during Jon's absence. Now that Natalie had explained, it all seemed so petty.

"Oh, yes. He's one hundred percent." She toyed some more with her croissant. "What do you think of him? Of Jon, I mean?"

I made a show of thinking it over. "He seems like a good man. A little distant, maybe. Remote."

"Ah, yes. Remote." She took a sip of coffee. "How much did he tell you about himself?"

Shifting uncomfortably on my seat, I thought it over before I spoke. "Well, I know he was married previously. I also know that his first wife...took her own life."

Natalie's eyebrows shot upward. "He told you that much? He must really like you. You look a little like her, you know."

I nodded.

"Did he take you anywhere? Out to dinner, maybe?"

"Yes," I admitted, wondering how much she knew. Was she testing me somehow?

"Where did you go?"

"To a little club by the ocean."

"Oh." She gave me a knowing nod. "I've been there myself. Interesting. Anywhere else?"

I hesitated, but when she raised one inquisitive eyebrow, I decided that I'd best be honest with her. "We spent an afternoon at his home on Biscayne Key. A woman named Vanessa and two of her friends came with us."

Natalie digested this information with a nod. Then she slapped the table and smiled. "I knew you were his type!"

"I don't understand."

"Ah, Demmie, I love my brother dearly. I love all of my brothers dearly. And I hate to see them make the wrong choices."

"And?" I hadn't the slightest idea what she meant.

"Vanessa Scorizio wants to become part of the Baxter family. She's been lobbying to make a match with Jon for a while. As I can't abide the woman, I'm thrilled that Jon took a liking to you."

I stared at her, my mouth agape.

She shrugged unapologetically. "Yes, I can be a bit of a matchmaker. But I have Jon's best interests at heart. A woman like Vanessa would never work out for him in the long run."

"You set me up with your brother?"

"I did. I pushed you at him, to see if he'd respond to you. You both have so much in common. Is that terrible of me?"

I slumped and gazed at my laptop, my thoughts whirling.

"Relax, darling," she said, and patted my hand a few times. "Were you at least a little intrigued by him?"

"More than intrigued," I choked out, amazed and despairing at the same time. "But you've misjudged him. He'll never allow himself to love me. Or anyone. He's shut away. Unavailable."

"That's what he says." A gleam brightened her eyes. "We'll see."

I grabbed my coffee cup with a trembling hand and took a sip.

"Did he fuck you?" she asked suddenly.

My heart gave a thump, and blood rushed anew into my cheeks. My face felt like it was on fire.

"I'm sorry," she quickly added. "I know I've got brass ones, asking you that."

"We were intimate," I admitted after a moment.

She clapped her hands together. "Perfect!"

"Perfect? How?"

"Perfect in that you've taken him from Vanessa for good. Jon never sleeps with more than one woman at once. Vanessa must be going out of her mind." She grinned triumphantly. "We've already won half the battle."

"I don't know anything about that." I gave her a glum look. "Jon and I are still employer and employee, no matter what you think."

"I'm going to be doing a lot of thinking," she agreed, a determined note in her voice. Then she focused on me with a singularly intense expression. "One of the reasons I agreed to hire you, Demmie, was because of your honesty. And your good heart. We investigated you thoroughly—"

I made a little noise of protest, but she held up her hand, effectively silencing me. "I know, we were intrusive, but I wanted to be sure. And now, I'm going to call upon your good heart, and ask you to honestly answer this question: Would you want more from my brother than sex, or money? Would his heart be safe in your hands? My instincts say yes, but I need to be sure."

My pulse pounding, I gave her a little nod.

"Do you love him already?" she asked.

I held my breath, unsure if I could truly trust her, and not quite believing things had gone in the direction they had. Finally, though, I could hold it no longer. I decided to take a chance. "Oh, God, yes," I gasped, and pressed a hand against my breast, to calm my heart. "I do love him. It happened so fast..."

She smiled perceptively. "Jon has that effect on women. And I promise you, darling, you wouldn't be sorry if a more permanent relationship developed between the two of you."

"But you hardly know me. How can you be so sure I'm right for him?"

"I'm an excellent judge of character, and I've seen enough," she replied firmly.

"But he told me himself I could expect nothing—"

"I know. He thinks he's quite shut off. He doesn't want to risk losing someone he loves. But I saw how he looked at you. It's a gleam in his eye I haven't seen for a long time." She patted my hand again. "I believe he's at least half in love with you already. We just need to make him see that if he doesn't act, he's again going to lose someone he loves. Will you play along with me?"

"I will," I agreed, and for the first time in two weeks, I was the one feeling a glimmer of hope.

□

CHAPTER THIRTEEN

True to her word, Natalie immediately embarked on a campaign to make Jon realize that he was going to lose me if he didn't take action. During the day, I worked on the various tasks she'd set me for our opening-night launch party, and at night she and I attended a round of dinners, parties, and clubs with a number of men she'd declared as 'eligible bachelors.' As per Natalie's instructions, I made sure to meet with Jon at least once a day to discuss business matters and, as painful as it was, rebuffed his more intimate invitations with the excuse of having previous plans with Natalie.

"Dinner tonight?" he'd ask.

And I would just shrug, and sadly shake my head no, and reply along the lines of, "I would love to, Jon, you know I would, but Natalie, she has me booked tonight. We're promoting the hotel launch, of course."

"Of course." With a frown, he'd stomp off. Clearly he wasn't used to rejection.

I could see his frustration with me growing as the days wore on, and even though I squirmed beneath his all-too-frequent glare, I stuck to my guns. Natalie insisted that her plan of making him feel like he was losing me would bring him to heel. I wasn't as certain, but nevertheless trusted that she understood her brother well enough to know what would work, and what wouldn't. And so, Natalie and I laughed and we flirted with numerous gorgeous men and none of it mattered a bit—I only wanted Jon, and I missed him. I wished he'd complain more, or corner me and demand my company, but he wasn't the asking kind, and I was under strict orders not to volunteer.

About a week before the opening-night launch party, we moved from the Barcelona to Beau Paradis. The changes that had been made to the hotel seemed miraculous to me—gone were the gaping holes in the roof, the trash, the broken pipes, the crumbling cement. The construction crews had worked miracles and had restored the hotel, which had once hosted such notables as Al Capone and Franklin D. Roosevelt, to a fanciful palace by the seaside, with terracotta-tiled roofs and reinforced concrete walls painted a warm yellow. Now it was an oasis of luxury amidst a subtropical forest...a dreamlike vision on the shores of Biscayne Bay...and its interior reflected all of its former glory with art-deco styling inspired by my Hollywood glamour idea.

I especially liked the lobby, with its soaring wall of art deco glass. When sunlight streamed through the glass, it painted the lobby with a brilliant rainbow of colors. It was in the lobby that I ran into Lucien Entrage again...or should I say, he ran into me.

"Demmie Phillps," he said, his voice low and intimate as he cornered me in a little nook not far from the front desk. He was just as tall and handsome as he'd been the previous time I'd seen him, and he had that same air of sophisticated conceit.

I drew in a quick, surprised breath. "Lucien."

He smiled. "You played quite a game with me last time we were together."

I glanced around, looking for a reason to ditch him, and hoping someone would see us.

He angled his body to make my escape impossible. "You seem distracted."

"I have a lot of things on my mind," I replied.

"I understand."

I gazed at him with some surprise. "You do?"

"You're concerned about the future."

"You might say that," I agreed. "Our opening-night gala is only two days away."

"I'll be there. I've booked the penthouse suite," he informed me. "But opening night isn't what really concerns you, is it?"

"I don't know what you mean."

He gave me a satisfied smile. "Baxter's with Vanessa Scorizio again. They've been seen around town. Where does that leave you?"

I stiffened. I hadn't heard this. Natalie hadn't mentioned it. Jon, back with Vanessa?

"Ah, I can see you didn't know. I'm sorry," he continued.

"You're very perceptive."

"I understand women."

"I'm certain you do." I inched away from him a little.

"Did you know that I'm a very wealthy man?"

"I guessed as much."

"Not as wealthy as Baxter, of course, but I'm very capable of setting a woman up in style: an oceanfront condo, beautiful clothes, jewelry, trips abroad, whatever she wants. Even plastic surgery," he bragged.

"How generous of you." I wondered if he knew what an ass he sounded like.

"I have other ways of keeping a woman satisfied, too."

"Oh, really?"

"I can provide references, if needed." He gave me a slow, seductive smile. "Even Vanessa Scorizio could provide a reference."

"So you've had her, too."

He shrugged. "She's a very beautiful woman. I like beautiful women."

"How flattering."

"I don't like how our last encounter ended, Demmie. I didn't know who you were." He leaned closer to me, until his breath fanned across my cheeks. "That would never happen again."

I frowned uneasily. "I'm sorry, but I'm not interested."

His face hardened. A muscle flexed in his jaw. His gray eyes became calculating. "If I remember correctly, you left with my money. One thousand dollars, to be exact. Don't you think I deserve to enjoy what I paid for?"

I froze. All at once I remembered the money he'd shoved into my evening bag—an evening bag I hadn't touched since that night. "Your money! I forgot. I don't want it. I'll go get it now—"

I tried to push past him, but he wrapped one large, strong hand around my arm and held me still. "I don't accept refunds."

I swiveled to stare at him, and I would have laughed, had I not seen the cold glint in his eyes.

He squeezed my arm once, for emphasis. "I plan on collecting on our debt. Be ready." With that, he turned and walked away from me, leaving me shivering in the corner.

The day of the hotel's opening-night gala dawned sunny and cool, with a breeze that would keep the temperatures down even further. I left my room and went down to the breakfast area set up to support the hotel's staff and heard angry voices coming out of the offices we used. Immediately I identified them as Natalie's and Jon's. I moved a little closer, determined to eavesdrop, and caught a glimpse of them through the doorway.

"Why the hell do you keep flaunting Demmie around Miami like a favorite niece? She has no time for anything but these parties of yours," Jon growled. I saw him waving his arms at his sister and crept back a little further. If he saw me...

"Now, Jon, I know she's our employee, but I've taken a shine to her," Natalie replied calmly. "She's young and naïve. It would be easy for her to get into trouble down here, among all these sharks. I'd just like to see her settled with the right man."

A brief pause. Then, Natalie continued, "I've heard some rumors, Jon. I don't want you toying with her. She's way too vulnerable."

He grunted. "Mind your own business."

"I won't," she declared. "If you mess with her, you mess with me."

"You and your matchmaking bullshit." I heard him stomping around the room. "You ought to start your own reality show."

A brief silence ensued, and I could imagine Natalie shrugging. "Demmie's certainly enjoying herself.

She's not complaining."

"I'll bet she isn't. Every night, you're parading her in front of someone new."

"What do you care? You're with that creature Vanessa," Natalie accused.

"It's completely platonic," he replied. "I wish I could say the same about Demmie and the men she's been hanging around."

"Really, Jon, to suggest that she's sleeping around...it's ridiculous."

"I know." His voice sounded gruff.

"Though I will admit," Natalie added, "she's quite charming. She turns more men down than you'd ever believe."

Jon grunted. Judging by the sound of his footsteps, he was still pacing. "Has she settled for anyone yet?"

Natalie sighed. "Not so far. She seems bored with them. I just can't shake the feeling that there's someone else she wants. Almost like an unrequited love that occupies her mind. It's quite sad, really."

Jon stopped pacing. "Has she said who she's thinking about?"

"No, it's just a gut feeling. Do you have any ideas who this mystery man might be?"

A beat of silence passed, and then I watched through the crack as Jon ran a hand through his hair.

She sighed. "It's no matter. With all the men I've introduced her to, she'll get over her mystery man soon enough."

"I'm sure she will," he agreed edgily, and marched toward the door. I had just enough time to turn away and rush into the ladies' room before he saw me. My hands shaking, I washed them beneath the beautiful gold fluted faucets, and stared at the dark pink stain on my cheeks, and the way my eyes gleamed.

Natalie was right. He was coming to heel. I felt like laughing aloud—with joy. But instead, I kept my composure, and went back to the office to finalize our preparations for the gala that night.

The moon rose high and full, and painted the waves with a silvery glow. Breakers rolled in and crashed on the sand with a rush of noise, but I could hardly hear them over the music and conversation that surrounded Beau Paradis. Workers had lifted white tents across the lawns and over the large patio area that faced the ocean, and placed wicker tables and chairs beneath the tents, in intimate little groupings. Flowers spilled from atop the tables, perfuming the air with their sweet scent, and lanterns strung along the edges of the tents like bunting offered a muted, intimate glow.

Over in the corner, a band played old-style music with a Latin flair, and bongos lent a throbbing beat that created a carnival-like atmosphere. Women dressed in silks and sequins, and men in tuxedos, either lounged on the chairs, or stood talking in loose circles. They were drinking the champagne that flowed freely from several different fountains, eating the many delicacies offered at the buffet, smoking cigarettes on long, slender holders, or puffing away at cigars. Old-style Hollywood red carpets covered the floors and led the partygoers from tent to tent, and posters of glamourous movie stars stood on easels in every corner. The feeling was lush and decadent.

From my position on a second-floor balcony, I

assessed it all with a critical eye and smiled. I couldn't have been happier with the way things had turned out. Moments later, Natalie joined me and expressed the same sentiment.

"Fabulous party, darling," she said.

I smiled. "I love it when everything goes according to plan."

We'd both chosen to wear black silk gowns that night, although hers showed decidedly more skin, and I wore the cornflower-blue silk scarf Jon had bought me. We'd also both styled our hair with a retro flair: Natalie looking like Ava Gardner, and me imitating Rita Hayworth. It was all marvelous fun, and when a photographer stopped by and asked for us to pose together for a few photographs, we draped ourselves in lazy poses and did our best to imitate bored stardom.

After he'd gone, Natalie searched the crowd with one raised eyebrow. "Have you seen Jon yet?"

I'd caught sight of him earlier from my balcony perch. Now, I glanced in that direction and found him once more. "He's over there," I said, and swallowed.

He'd never been more handsome, more dazzling than he was tonight in a Tom Ford suit, which Natalie had explained was styled specifically to evoke a sense of 1940's sophistication. His jacket, a plain black with two buttons in the front and double-vented for style and movement, had been superbly cut to emphasize his physique; and the plain trousers encased his long, muscular legs in simple elegance. His shirt was clean, crisp, and ice-white, with a high collar that emphasized his strong, square jaw and tanned skin. He'd brushed his tawny hair back from his forehead and dressed it with a light pomade, and boldly wore the gold hoop earring in his left ear, as any pirate would. Oh, yes, he was dazzling...an absolute spectacle of masculine beauty.

I shifted my attention to one of Jon's heavily-muscled bodyguards, who stood nearby, casually surveying the crowd. I knew the bodyguard was looking for potential threats to his employer's well-being and had to shake my head. What danger could possibly exist here, of all places—at this very private party, with only the richest in attendance?

"Jon will be looking for you tonight," she predicted. "I've no doubt he'll want to dance with you. I spoke to him earlier, and I'm telling you, he's like a hound with a scent in his nose—your scent. You've given him a merry chase, darling, and when he finally wins you, the prize will be that much more valuable to him."

I wanted to laugh at the way Natalie insisted on comparing her brother—billionaire Jon Baxter--to a dog. Still, my own impatience at having to play this game, when all I wanted to do was throw myself into his arms, kept the laughter stuck in my throat. "Are you certain this is working? I've hardly spent any time at all with him over the last two weeks—"

"Trust me," she insisted. "It's a classic matchmaking strategy, and it's never failed me. When you increase the challenge, you increase the value...and force him to consider the possibility that he could lose out if he isn't careful. And believe me, he's considering."

"Can I dance with him, at least, if he asks me?"

"Of course." Natalie gave me an insistent tap on the arm. "Just make sure he sees you dancing with plenty of other men, too."

Luckily for me, I hadn't much trouble satisfying Natalie's request for me to dance with as many other men as possible that night. With her supporting me, I'd become a hot commodity on the Miami singles scene: young, hip, working for a high-powered real estate company, 'in' with the company owners, largely responsible for the marketing and promotion of a five-star hotel launch. When I wasn't checking with the caterers, the band, and anyone else who needed some sort of decision made, I was dancing on the patio with one of several different rich, successful bachelors and more than a few married men, too. Lucien Entrage, who'd also showed up, was the only man who I turned down...and this I did with a shiver, when I saw the antagonism in his gray eyes—antagonism, and something much hungrier.

By the time midnight rolled around, my feet ached and my head buzzed with too much champagne. I'd spent so much time smiling that my face felt permanently frozen into a happy expression. But the fact that Jon had yet to ask me to dance bugged me the most. He'd danced once with Vanessa, who continued to hang all over him, and had taken to the floor a few more times with a few of Miami's older society matrons. Other than that, though, he'd seemed content to linger on the edge of the dance floor, watching me and frowning.

After our intimacy, it felt so strange to have this wall between us, this artificial distance, one his sister had engineered for the sole sake of drawing us closer, through some sort of reverse psychology. I wanted to go to him, to put my arms around him and kiss him in full view of anyone who cared to watch...including Vanessa, who seemed oblivious to the fact that he only gave her half his attention. But I stuck to my agreement with Natalie and waited for him to come to me, to ask me to dance, and to hopefully conclude this chase that had consumed us both for weeks now.

And so, it was with a great deal of joy that I accepted a small piece of paper sometime after midnight in Jon's looping scrawl, asking me to come upstairs to the second-floor suite, the one we'd been using as a temporary office. As soon as I read it, I glanced toward the last place I'd seen Jon lingering, and noticed Vanessa, but not him. He must, I thought, be waiting for me inside.

The fact that he wanted to see me in our offices tempered my excitement somewhat, and made me think that he had some business issue he wanted to discuss. Then again, I told myself...the hour was well past midnight, so what business could possibly interest him other than that of kissing me? My heart suddenly beating double-time, I spun away from the patio and hurried into the lobby.

Inside, the place was deserted. Even the skeleton staff we'd hired to mind the hotel while the gala was underway had gathered outside to watch the fireworks, which would shortly be set off on the beach. My high heels clicking on the marble floor, I raced towards the staircase, through the murky yellow-orange light coming from antique sconces. The fountain we'd had installed against one wall spurted water that gurgled as it made its way down to the drain, but otherwise the lobby remained silent.

For some reason, that silence suddenly seemed

ominous. I had a sense of being watched. I slowed my steps and looked around. A clock on the wall ticked out the seconds and, outside, the boom of the first cannon announced the start of the fireworks show. The band started a new, lively number and a shower of light flashed above the beach. It penetrated the stained-glass window, to create sparks of multi-colored light across the lobby.

Everything seemed normal. And yet, a feeling of oppression hung over me. I fought an urge to run and hide in the shadows, and creep through the rest of the lobby on bare feet.

Stop being so silly, I told myself. Jon was upstairs, waiting for me--

Just then, Lucien Entrage stepped out from behind the fountain and stood looking at me.

I froze. My pulse jumped. Lucien assessed me boldly, without bothering to hide the hostility in his gaze. He looked as big as a tree and just as solid in his black tuxedo, with his black hair falling carelessly over his brow. Like Jon, he was a beautiful specimen of male virility, but while Jon had an air of decency about him, Lucien's face twisted with ruthlessness. He gave me a mocking, sardonic smile that turned my blood to ice.

"Going somewhere?" he asked, his voice much too polite.

I clutched Jon's note in my hand. "Mr. Baxter and I have some business to discuss—"

"In the second-floor office suite?" he cut in.

I stared uneasily at him.

His smile became satisfied.

It took a second for his meaning to sink in and, when it did, my lips parted. I quickly scanned the note again. "But it's in Jon's handwriting—"

"Not so hard to forge," he observed. "I wanted to see you. I knew that would bring you in here."

I looked at the front door. "I have to go back."

"You will stay."

I took a stumbling step backward. I'd worked so hard to make this gala perfect, that the last thing I wanted to do was yell for help, or otherwise create a scene—with Lucien Entrage, no less.

He took a few steps toward me.

I glanced toward the front desk, then out at the patio. Someone would return in a moment.

"They're all out watching the fireworks," he observed.

"I'll scream," I threatened.

"Go ahead." He moved closer.

I backed up until I was against the wall. My knees wobbled. "What do you want?"

"You played me for a fool, and then took my money."

"I never took your money," I babbled. "You shoved it in my evening bag. And you drugged me."

"You're not going to trick me again," he informed me, and stopped about two feet away. "Not tonight, and not ever. Tonight I'm going to put you in your place."

"And just where is that?"

"On your back, with your legs spread, like the little slut you are."

I stared at him, horrified, as a slow, evil smile spread across his lips. His eyes were glowing like dark, hot coals; and when I glanced down at his trousers, I saw an enormous bulge between his legs. I pushed harder against the wall. "Stay away."

"Maybe I ought to fuck you right here, in the lobby. I'll take you hard, and make you squirm and squeal beneath me. You'd like that, wouldn't you?"

I cast a terrified glance toward the patio. Please, please someone come in...

"I've been planning this for a while," he chatted. "Ever since that day you left me in the cabana--hard up, so to speak. Do you know what I had to do, after you left with your employer? I had to find a waitress. I brought her into the cabana and threw her onto the bed and took her by force. She squealed so much that I had to cover her mouth with my hand. I did this because I couldn't have you."

"You disgust me," I choked out, my throat dry.

Another round of fireworks exploded on the beach, and the music swelled again. Beneath it, I thought I heard someone calling my name, a faint, barely audible sound that could have been a stray moment of conversation.

He chuckled, low in his throat. "She was a little slut like you. She was begging for it, and she got what she deserved." He paused and drew an ivory-handled pocket knife from his jacket. Casually, he flicked it open. The blade gleamed, its edge silvery and sharp. "After we were done, I nicked her throat with a knife—drew a little blood—and told her that if she said anything about this to anyone, the next cut would be a lot deeper."

He moved a step nearer, his eyes glittering with brutal lust, and lifted a curl from my shoulder. He looked at it, another jeering smile curving his lips, then settled it back against my skin. I could see from the glint in his eyes that he was relishing my fear, my powerlessness; so I returned his stare with a stoic one of my own—no way would I let him see me sweat.

Suddenly, his movements swift and sure, he grabbed my arm and shoved it up behind my back.

I cried out, but then his hot, sweaty palm was covering my mouth. I bit at his flesh, and he cursed as he hustled me sideways, toward a service corridor that led back toward the kitchen. I stumbled and tripped and was a dead weight against him as he dragged me. I could feel his erection, hot and as hard as steel, pressing against my side.

"I'm going to use you like I used the waitress," he hissed against my ear. "You're going to get it hard, sweetheart, and then you're going to lick my boots. Understand?"

I twisted wildly against him, sunk my teeth into his palm again.

He yanked his hand away from me. "Goddamn little slut," he growled, then cuffed me on the side of the head. Stars exploded in my field of vision. I swayed. Everything was going black. I felt him grab the back of my dress, heard it rip. Then he had me by the neck. He kept me on my feet, shuffled me backward.

And then, without warning, we stopped moving. For a few seconds that seemed to stretch into an eternity, we just stood there.

"Let her go."

The voice came from nowhere. It was firm, low, and full of menace. I opened my eyes—everything looked wavy. I saw a tall man in a tuxedo standing several feet away. His hair glimmered with tawny highlights.

Jon!

A mountainous form stood next to Jon. He'd

brought his bodyguard with him.

"Let her go, Entrage," Jon calmly advised, and took a step nearer to us.

"She has a debt to satisfy," my tormentor said, his voice steady as he shuffled me away a few steps.

"How much does she owe you?" Jon took several bills from his wallet and threw them on the floor between us. "There's ten thousand dollars."

Jon's bodyguard circled around to the left and crept closer.

"This isn't about money anymore." Lucien swung me around and held me hostage-style. "Tell your goon to stand back." I felt a slicing pain at my neck, and then the warmth of dripping blood. I knew then that Lucien had nicked me, just like he'd nicked the waitress.

"Stephen," Jon murmured. His large companion moved backwards.

I felt Lucien relax a little, his grip loosening. The knife no longer pressed against my skin. "Good," he said. "Now both of you, back off. Go outside and enjoy the party."

Jon nodded, seemingly at ease now. "Fine. Just make sure I get her back undamaged."

I felt rather than saw Lucien grin in response. "Don't worry. I won't spoil your fun—"

With a quickness that amazed me, Jon surged forward and dove toward Lucien, bringing him down even as he freed me from Lucien's steel-like grip. I sprawled away and stared, horrified, as the two men grappled on the floor, the knife between them. Jon's bodyguard raced forward, a gun drawn in his hand, but the two men were struggling so fiercely that a shot could just as easily hit Jon as Lucien.

But then, Jon wrestled the knife from Lucien and whipped his hand around. The blade flashed in the light as Jon drove it savagely into Lucien's gut. Lucien shuddered convulsively and made a horrible gurgling sound, then went limp and dropped to the ground as Jon released his grip. The whole thing happened so quickly, it took me a second to make sense of what I'd seen.

Stunned, I stared at the blood, listened to the groans Lucien was making, and then gazed dumbly at Jon, who seemed completely at ease with the situation. He leaned forward and held a hand out to me. My fingers shaking, I grasped his palm and allowed him to haul me to my feet. He pulled me against his body and held me there, as my knees shook and nearly collapsed beneath me. "You really know how to get yourself into trouble," he murmured.

I swayed dizzily and trembled. I wondered if this was a nightmare I would shortly wake up from. And yet, the feel of Jon's hand gripping my arm, and the hard, muscled length of his body pressed against mine, reassured me that this was no nightmare.

Frowning, Jon took off his jacket and put it over my shoulders. Then he glanced at his bodyguard, who was returning his gun to the holster hidden beneath his jacket. "Take care of this, will you, Stephen?"

The bodyguard nodded and moved to Lucien's side.

Jon curled an arm around my waist and held me close. "I'm bringing you upstairs, to my room."

I reveled in Jon's nearness, in the feel of his muscular arm clasping me against him, in his deliciously masculine smell, something soapy and spicy at the same time. "Did you kill him?" I whispered, with a glance at Lucien.

"I don't think so. God knows he deserved it, though."

We shuffled through the hotel lobby just as the third, and final, set of fireworks boomed over the ocean. I rested my head against his shoulder and felt his strength, his warmth, as well as the tension in his body as we entered the elevator. In a few seconds we were getting off at the first floor and heading toward the suite he'd claimed for himself during the final weeks of renovations.

We walked down the hall and paused in front of the door to his suite. He used a key-card to open the door.

"How did you find me?" I asked, as we lurched inside.

"I had my eye on you all night," he said, his lips brushing against my ear lobe. "Wouldn't you know that the one second I left to check on my sister, you disappeared?"

The door shut behind us, and then he pulled me into his arms and crushed me tightly, yet tenderly against him, rocking me gently as he pressed little kisses against the top of my head. The doors to his balcony stood open, and beyond, the fireworks danced over the ocean, bringing with them a smoky, acrid odor. He kissed me, his lips warm and seeking, while outside, the partygoers exclaimed with delight.

I opened my mouth almost blindly to his, returned his kiss and then began to cry. Tears streamed down my cheeks.

His arms tightened around me. "Shhh," he murmured. "You're with me, now."

"I know," I sobbed. I was falling apart.

He wiped my tears away, and held me, and rocked me, and kissed me.

We stayed like that until the last of the fireworks had faded away. Throughout it all, I clung to him and fought back fresh waves of tears; and when the band began playing a quiet melody, I looked into his loving eyes and knew everything was going to be okay.

"Thank God you looked in the lobby," I whispered, between hiccups.

"It was the first place I went," he replied. We moved over to the bed. Carefully he sat me down, and then swung my feet up. When he started to pull my dress up over my head, I shrunk away from him a little, but then reminded myself that this was Jon, not Lucien, and the fear melted away.

Jon finished taking the dress off of me, and tucked a sheet over me. Then he walked around the bed, his gaze on me, before he crouched down against the wall and sighed, deeply. "I need to tell you some things. To explain."

"Okay," I agreed tremulously.

"My father and mother, they didn't have a lot of money," he began. "We lived near the beach, in a little house. My father, he was a handyman. He taught my brothers and me how to fix things. We live in a throw-away culture, but he showed us the thrill of reclaiming old things."

He paused, and I sensed he was digging deep into his memory, and recalling past hurts that would always be difficult for him to talk about.

"I had friends, of course," he continued, "but my best friend was Sarah. She lived next door. She liked to fix things too, and she had a way with animals.

Birds with broken wings, mice caught in traps—she fixed them. She didn't reclaim old things, she brought things back from death." He sighed, and his shoulders seemed to cave in a little. "But her connection with death was too strong. When one of her birds died, she despaired. I didn't see it then, but with each animal she lost, she sank deeper into depression."

He stood up suddenly, and sat down next to me on the bed. "My brothers and I worked day and night. When I was sixteen, we pooled our money together and bought an old hotel in the worst section of town. We fixed it up and opened it. It did well, so we bought two more hotels. And then a few more. And while we were growing richer, Sarah stayed at my side. After a while, we married. She busied herself with charities and fundraisers, but I knew she was depressed.

And as before, she still tried to fix things, to snatch things from death. Death became her old friend. When she lost our baby mid-term, it was too much for her. So she followed in the path of so many of the things she'd loved."

"She killed herself," I whispered.

He nodded, his face tight. "Afterwards, I didn't speak for months. Stayed in the house for a long time. My brothers thought I was going to kill myself too. But I was afraid to kill myself. I didn't have the relationship with death that she'd had. To me, death was darkness. It was chaos. I realized that I'd spent my entire married life fighting death." He sagged a little more. "It took me a long time to let her go."

"And when you did," I added, "you also buried your heart away. Refused to allow anyone to get close to you, for fear of being hurt again."

He cast an appreciative glance my way. "That's right. Keeping myself apart from others became a way of life." Words seemed to fail him then. He trailed off and looked out the balcony, and the darkness beyond. The fireworks had finished, and all that remained was a heavy mantle of smoke which drifted ever closer to the ocean.

I grabbed his hand, held it. "If you want me, you have to open your heart."

He turned to lock gazes with me, his eyes brimming with an emotion I couldn't name.

"You have to let yourself feel. To trust, to hope again."

He nodded. "The day you came into my life, Demmie, everything changed. You were so quiet, so innocent, and so sweet, I didn't even see you coming. Somehow, though, you snuck beneath my defenses and stole a heart that I didn't even realize I possessed."

I sucked in a little breath. Tears pricked the back of my eyes.

"I had loved Sarah, yes," he said, his voice throbbing with feeling. "But now, I realize that my love for her had always been dark, brooding, filled with doubt and shadow. Worrying over her fascination with death had caused me nothing but anxiety."

I gripped his hand harder, tried to give him strength to finish it, to tell me what he hid in his heart.

"You, though," he breathed, his eyes gleaming. "Where Sarah had been an exercise in darkness and futility, you're light, you're vitality. From the very first moment I saw you, I basked in your enthusiasm, your joy for life. Obsessed by that fear Sarah had taught me, I fought the love I felt for you, with every ounce of strength I had. I fought it, denied it...until I saw you with Lucien's knife at your throat and it exploded in front of me like a revelation."

He let out a long, shuddering breath and clasped my hand with his other free one. "And now, that I have you safe in my arms, I want you there always. Do you want to stay, Demmie? Or have I already driven you away?"

Feeling like the most fortunate woman alive, I smiled with a joy that was all the more blessed for having almost been denied. "You must be blind. I've loved you from the first moment I saw you, in the Barcelona's lobby. As long as you'll have me, I'm not going anywhere."

He leaned forward, scooped me into his arms and crushed me to him. "My God, when I think about how close I came to losing you..."

"You haven't lost me, Jon. I'm here, and always will be."

Our lips met and he gave me a long, lazy kiss, his mouth lingering over mine as his arms tightened and he drew me closer still. I twined my hands around his neck, and then ran my fingers into his thick hair, stroking and tangling and tugging gently. He moaned deep in his throat and swung me around in his arms, until I was on top of him and our lazy kiss became harder, more demanding, and I shivered with the delicious sensations he aroused in me, feelings that had never been quite this sweet.

He turned his head and looked into my eyes, his own a deep, deep blue filled with urgent love. I caressed his cheek with my fingers, ran them along the bridge of his nose, and slid them along his lips, before gently pressing my mouth to his and tenderly expressing the love for him that trembled inside.

I'd waited a long time for this moment. I'd thought about it, dreamed about it...and now, as he began exploring my body with eager hands that so effortlessly provoked a soul-searing bliss...I lived it. We kissed, caressed, skin against skin, mouth against flesh, filled each other, became one, probing, deeper, then deeper still, until a shimmering, shattering radiance lifted us both high into a joyous oblivion so rarely reached.

Afterwards, I snuggled in his arms, and he nibbled my earlobe, his eyes a smoldering blue now.

"I'll bet Natalie's wondering what happened to us," I murmured.

He nuzzled my neck. "Let her wonder."

"She's going to be so happy when she finds out we're together. She's been trying to make it happen for weeks now," I admitted, the marvelous glow he'd created inside me banked, for now.

'She's going to be impossible to live with. I'm sure she'll be planning our wedding before the week is out."

I chuckled and fitted myself more closely into the crook of his arm. "Are you asking me to marry you?"

"I am."

"I'll have to think about it."

He ran his hand along my naked butt, then gave it a little smack.

I yelped with pretended pain. "Okay, I thought about it. Yes!"

"That's my girl," he breathed, and then he was

kissing me again.

ABOUT THE AUTHOR…

Georgina Sand lives by day as a buttoned-up corporate type, writing technical specifications, analyzing processes and data, going to nerd conventions and eating the same lunch every day in the company cafeteria.

By night, however, it's an entirely different story—she ditches the flat shoes and business suit, and cuddles up with her laptop and a glass of wine to write stories that are wicked hot and sometimes kinky, but always inventive and full of emotion. She adores sensuality, high heels and travel; and her dearest wish is to make her readers purr and feel like they're there, in the story, experiencing it themselves.

For more from Georgina:

http://georginasand.com/

www.ingramcontent.com/pod-product-compliance
Lightning Source LLC
Chambersburg PA
CBHW021035130626
46552CB00005B/1848

* 9 7 8 0 6 9 2 4 4 8 7 7 9 *